More Critical Praise for Salar Abdoh

for *Out of Mesopotamia*

"If history is written by the victors then most good war novels are written by those accustomed to losing, and *Out of Mesopotamia* calls to mind the grim brilliance of Czech writers like Bohumil Hrabal and Jaroslav Hasek—which is to say it is really fucking funny. And maybe this is at the heart of Abdoh's genius, the art and instinct for getting very close to the darkest corners of humanity without succumbing to the despair that dwells therein."
—*Literary Hub*

"*Out of Mesopotamia* is extraordinary and a novel every American should read. Salar Abdoh writes page after page of kinetic fiction. A novel so ambitious and exciting—to say this book is full of truth is to shortchange it; this is a book full of art."
—*Aster(ix)*

"Abdoh's superb meditation on art and war exploits and subverts the tropes of popular Western war novels for a thrilling, sometimes comical ride through a horrific series of battles."
—*Publishers Weekly*, a Best Book of the Year selection

"Transcendent."
—*Daily Beast*

"[A]s much a meditation on time and memory as it is a book about war ... Abdoh skillfully captures combat's intrinsic absurdity ... For many Americans, the conflicts in Syria and Iraq have become abstractions, separated from our lives by geographic as well as psychic boundaries. Abdoh collapses these boundaries, presenting a disjointed reality in which war and everyday life are inextricably entwined ... [The novel shines] a brilliant, feverish light on the nature of not only modern war but all war, and even of life itself."
—*New York Times Book Review*

"Abdoh takes heavy subjects and themes and presents them with a deft, light hand ... *Out of Mesopotamia* nearly produces an out of body reading experience as it transports the reader to the war zones the author toured, while capturing the inherent beauty and strangeness present in both war and art."
—*Markaz Review*

for *Tehran at Twilight*

"[A] swift, hard-boiled novel . . . Shadowy zealots exist everywhere, whether in conference rooms or interrogation rooms or—most often—in rooms that can serve as both."   —*New York Times Book Review*

"Abdoh paints a gripping portrait of a nation awash in violence and crippled by corruption . . . Captivating."   —*Publishers Weekly*

"A smart political thriller for our modern times."
—Laila Lalami, author of *The Other Americans*

"Abdoh . . . gives readers a visceral sense of life in a country where repression is the norm, someone is always watching, and your past is never really past. Recommended for espionage aficionados and for readers who enjoy international settings."   —*Library Journal*

"A fascinating glimpse of contemporary Iran through the familiar story of childhood friends whose paths are beginning to diverge irreversibly."
—*Shelf Awareness*

 "A penetrating look into contemporary Tehran."   —*Kirkus Reviews*

"Salar Abdoh is an acute observer of the patterns, flaws, and simple beauties of everyday life . . . [*Tehran at Twilight* is] an unpretentious, cross-cultural political thriller that rings true in the way only a skillfully crafted novel can."   —*San Francisco Book Review*

"Abdoh's restraint with the brutality in present-day Iran in no way tamps down the adrenalin that keeps his characters in action . . . Goodness and mercy eventually carry the day, within limits, and this relatively new author already may have potential readers looking forward to his next novel."   —*Buffalo News*

"New history and a fresh take on the same old dirty tricks result in a clever and compelling tale."   —*National* (UAE)

"Abdoh is superb . . . *Tehran at Twilight* is an impressive work of fiction . . . Abdoh's talent is obvious from the first scene in the story until the bittersweet end."   —*CounterPunch*

Mehri Rahmzadeh

SALAR ABDOH was born in Iran and splits his time between Tehran and New York City. He is the author of the novels *Tehran at Twilight*, *The Poet Game*, and *Opium*; and he is the editor of *Tehran Noir*. He teaches in the MFA program at the City College of New York.

OUT OF
MESOPOTAMIA

OUT OF MESOPOTAMIA

BY Salar Abdoh

AKASHIC
BOOKS
BROOKLYN, NEW YORK

Published by Akashic Books
©2020, 2022 Salar Abdoh

Paperback ISBN: 978-1-63614-032-2
Hardcover ISBN: 978-1-61775-860-7
Library of Congress Control Number: 2020935751

Akashic Books
Brooklyn, New York
Instagram, Twitter, Facebook: AkashicBooks
E-mail: info@akashicbooks.com
Website: www.akashicbooks.com

*This book owes a debt of gratitude to Ibrahim Ahmad—
editor, friend, interlocutor. And it is dedicated to the
noble people of the Land Between the Two Rivers.*

To see both blended in one flood,
The mother's milk, the children's blood . . .

—Richard Crashaw, "Upon the Infant Martyrs"
(1646)

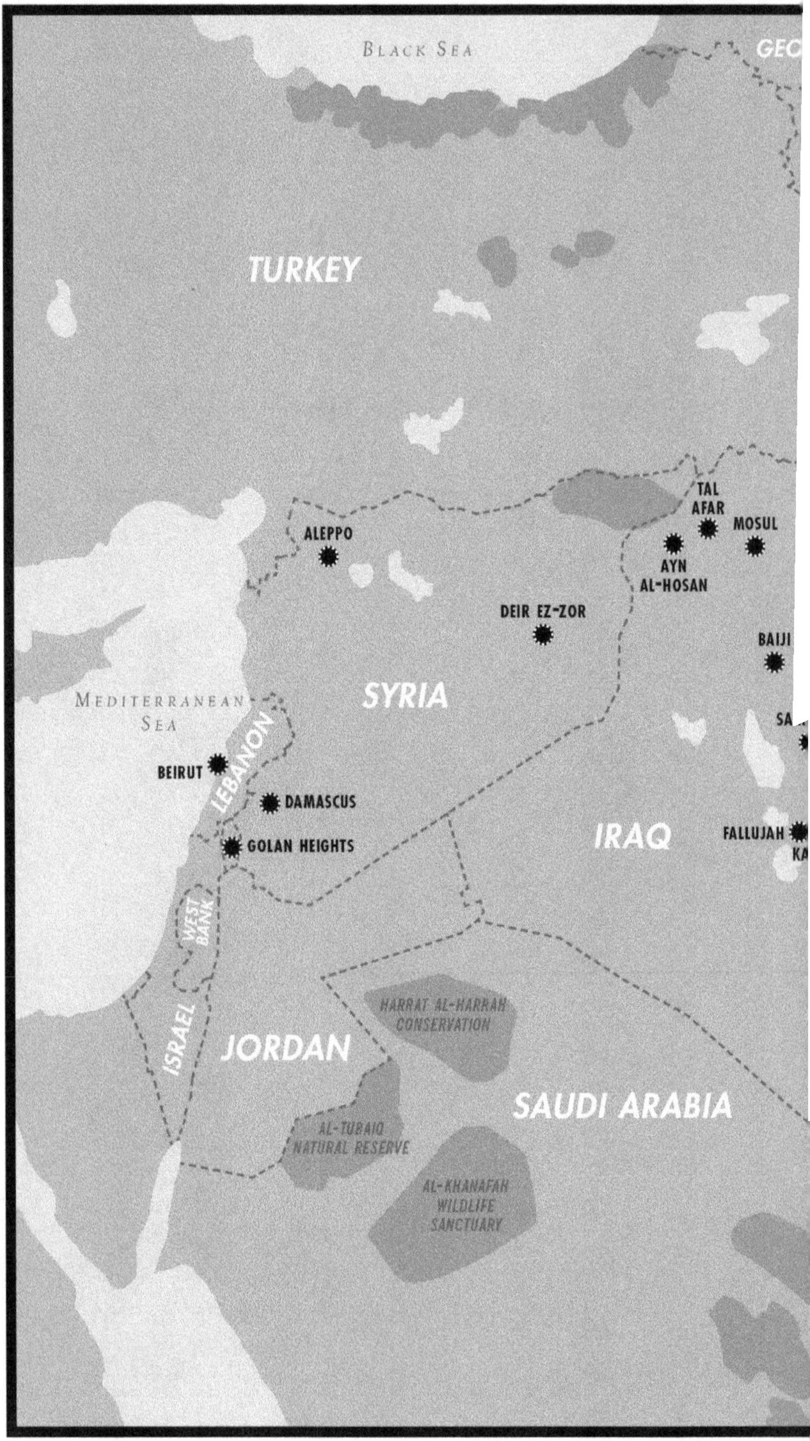
BLACK SEA
TURKEY
TAL AFAR
MOSUL
ALEPPO
AYN AL-HOSAN
DEIR EZ-ZOR
BAIJI
MEDITERRANEAN SEA
SYRIA
BEIRUT
LEBANON
DAMASCUS
GOLAN HEIGHTS
IRAQ
FALLUJAH
WEST BANK
HARRAT AL-HARRAH CONSERVATION
ISRAEL
JORDAN
SAUDI ARABIA
AL-TUBAIQ NATURAL RESERVE
AL-KHANAFAH WILDLIFE SANCTUARY

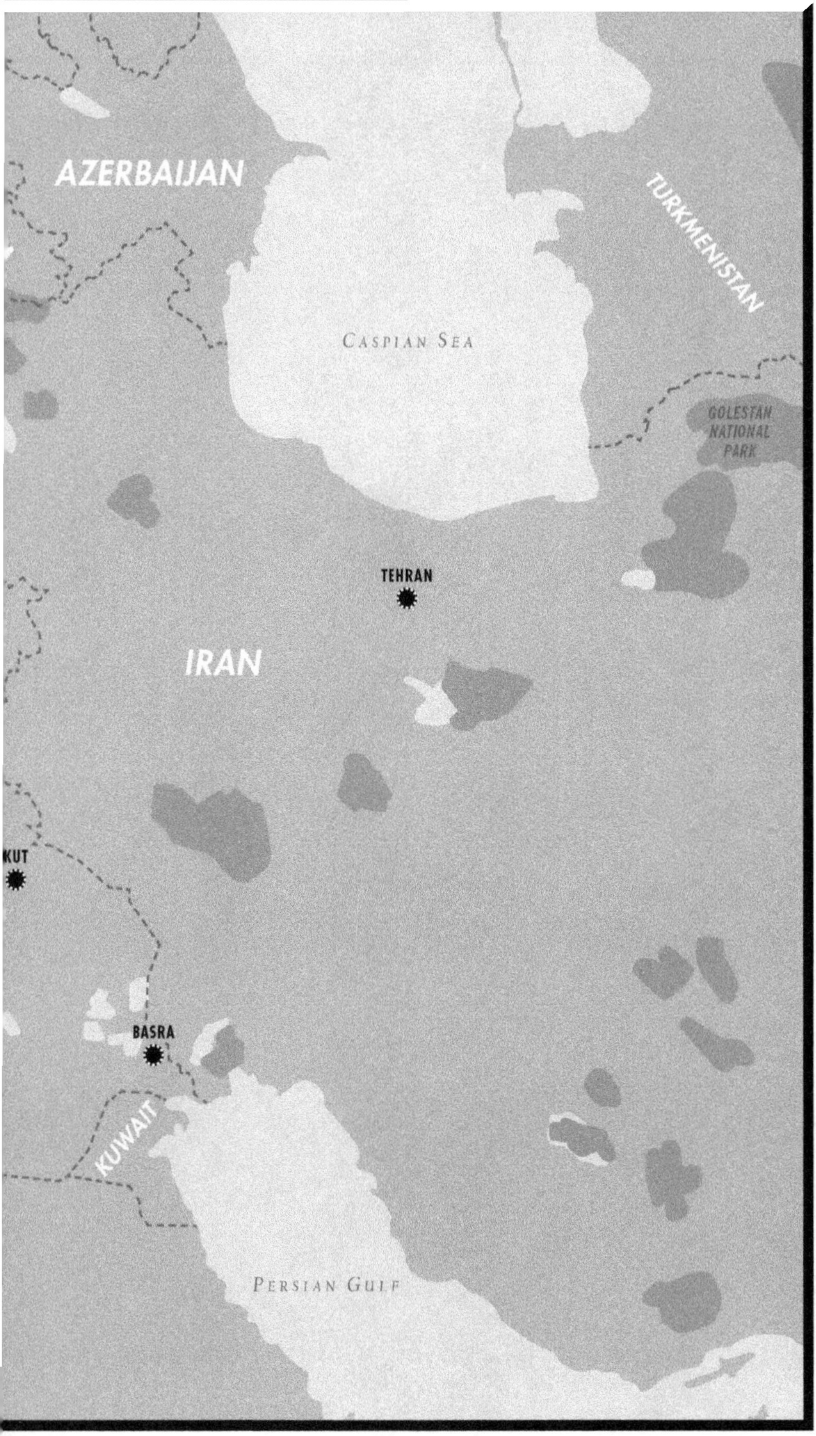
AZERBAIJAN
TURKMENISTAN
CASPIAN SEA
GOLESTAN
NATIONAL
PARK
TEHRAN
IRAN
KUT
BASRA
KUWAIT
PERSIAN GULF

1

Nasif held an index finger to his lips, hushing himself and me. I didn't see this but felt it, because he did it often, especially when the Afghans of his company got excited. The men who wanted to kill us were glued to the ground somewhere out there. Nasif was a sure shot and I was as good as blind in the dark. Like a lot of people there, his was a nom de guerre—for reasons of security, they said, though I was certain it was of no consequence what false name a soldier used. In fact, we had to call him not just Nasif, but Abu Nasif. But I'll make it simple here, as there were entire armies of men in the battlefields of Mesopotamia who were called Abu-something. This purely Arabic designation, Abu—*father*—did not suit the majority of them, though; they were too young to be fathers. So when they died, which was often, the title turned into a butterfly, transitory, and it went on to perch on somebody else who was new to the war and still breathing.

Usually not for long.

Together, Nasif and I made a questionable night watch. But those specters, I was sure, were out there, digital contours inside Nasif's neck-breaking night vision gadget in the vast Syrian blackness. I'd only seen them in daytime, as body parts or dead. At nights I'd hear them. Until now I had done everything to come farther west. Begged mostly. Because I wanted to report on the fight at its fiercest. But my half blindness made me a liability. Not a huge one, because honestly this war was on the side of clumsy. And now I just wanted to go back east again, back to Iraq, where it was safe. This safeness was relative. It only meant that over there you knew who your enemy was. Here, in Syria, it was different. Here lurked true evil.

I sat back. Nasif, who had been ghostly silent for the last hour, had an affected Afghan accent. Sometimes when we were alone he would forget and shift into his regular Persian of the northeast of Iran. There was a noticeable difference. Yet I didn't bother calling him out on his act. He did it because the Revolutionary Guards, who were in charge of all logistics and combat operations, were not so keen on just any Iranian getting up to come way out here. There had to be some form of control. Our Afghan mercenaries they could control. There was a command structure. Regular military accountability. There were paychecks and leaves. With Iranians it was different. Pay for combat was the last thing these guys came here for. Mostly they came because they wanted martyrdom. I will try to convey what this means: this fucking hunger for martyrdom that grips a man, or woman, and won't let them go. I will fail entirely at explaining it, of course, because in the end it's the one thing that is unexplainable. But I'll try anyway. Because I've seen it, tasted it from a safe but close enough distance.

I figured that Nasif, who had bought himself a counterfeit Afghan identity and practiced the accent to pass muster, was now in his element here in nowhereland, ready to die and have a street or a traffic circle named after him back home.

And die, he would. Very soon. Yet he would never be graced with the glory of a thoroughfare dedicated in his real name, or even the fake one. Nasif's calculations were wrong; he would not become a celebrated martyr.

In the meantime, while he was still alive, I questioned his sanity.

And my own.

The enemy was so close now I could hear them breathe *God is great* even before they said it; sometimes you actually hear a man say *Allahu akbar* before the utterance. You can feel the fear in him; he's pumping himself up, charging every fiber of his wasted life, knowing the chances that he'll get to you are not very good. Because you are almost as determined as he is. Almost. You feel him and hate him. There were men here who said this particular enemy was just misled, deluded. They said, "Kill them because you have to, but don't hate them. They are, after all, fellow believers who only went astray." But being evenhanded is not an easy thing. I hated a lot of things. I hated not being here more than I hated being here.

This was a dilemma.

But the bigger dilemma was our makeup, ours and the enemy's. They had descended like locusts on this land to establish God's rule while carrying out suicide attacks on civilians just about everywhere else. They were unforgiving in both pursuits, and they came from every continent. From day one they possessed a fearsome arsenal that seemed to have materialized out of thin air, and they went by a variety of names. Western news agencies mostly just called them the Islamic State. I'll stick to *enemy*.

Enemy spoke a Babel of languages. We, on the other hand, who were there to stop them, mostly just spoke Arabic and Persian. The Afghans among us were formidable warriors, maybe by virtue of how much fighting they'd known since the beginning of time. But they were hired hands in the end. They did not get dreamy-eyed about martyrdom like the Iranians did. The Iranians, us, who hired the Afghans for the job and shared the wistful and fragile sounds of Persian with them, did get dreamy-eyed. In fact, there was a degree of dreaminess about the Iranians that sometimes made you think the world would go to sleep one day and simply forget to wake up.

We were also hitting outside of our comfort zone. Syria and Iraq were deep Arab lands that may have needed us just then to stop the enemy. But they didn't want us. They didn't love us. Yet we were there, equipped with some bullshit reason about protecting the holy sites of Mesopotamia from the desecrations of the common enemy. This made us suspect, even to ourselves. And often I wondered if our pretense was not worse than that of the Americans, who variously dropped bombs on the enemy and on us and put it all down to saving civilization.

At least the Americans, for all their bluster and spine-chilling gunships, did not cram belief down anyone's throat.

We did.

Or we tried.

* * *

Lately, the red house had been a favorite obsession for the enemy. By now the initial suspicion that the regulars had for me had settled into a stolid acceptance, even deference. The Iraqi Arabs who were there called me Doctor, the Iranians called me Professor, while the Afghans preferred Commander. None of this was said with irony. We were all getting shot at equally and dying at farcical rates; distrust under these circumstances doesn't have a place and the mortars and DShK rounds make no distinction. Nasif had come a week before our night watch, asking for volunteers for the red house. The enemy was desperate to get it back, and there was something absurd about this desire of theirs. Even more absurd was their drive to get back the town of Khan-T in which the red house sat. Maybe they thought they could relink with the road to Aleppo from there and pause their recent losing streak. Whatever it was, they were dying for it, which suited us.

Nasif said, "The red house is empty."

The rage in his voice was contained but icy. In that simple statement I saw all the strangeness of this war. What were we doing here? Vultures perched on Mesopotamia's tired bones. I glimpsed Moalem, who was my age, a hardened veteran of the Iran-Iraq War of thirty-odd years earlier, wheezing and writing in his notebook. He couldn't write a war diary if his mother's life depended on it. But I wasn't going to tell him that. More than anyone he'd warmed up to me, reminiscing about how the Karbala-4 battle of back in the day was the mother of all battles—though he should have said mother of all defeats. He lost two cousins and three dozen comrades in that bleak epic. Maybe it was there where he was gassed; I never asked him about it and he didn't offer details. Moalem wheezed and gradually died over these thirty years, yet he kept at it. War for him was a kind of essence. He breathed it. Without it he ceased to be. Moalem too, like Nasif, would soon be dead. I would not be here at Khan-T when it happened. They'd bring me four of his notebooks filled with daily minutiae of war in Syria, tasking me to edit them into something comprehensible for publication. They were mostly banal observations about weapons: The 120 mortar. The 60. The lethal, unavoidable Kornet, which they said eventually killed him. Lot of scribbling about his faith and the faith of his companions in those pages. He wrote about fasting for days on end when there was not much else to do here, about going to Damascus to pay his respects at the Zaynab shrine. He wrote about martyrdom and never let up on that subject. Martyrdom was our shibboleth; we distinguished each other's sincerity by the way someone talked too little or too much about it. We knew who was lying and who was telling the truth when they prayed for martyrdom. We were adept at intuiting when a guy was ready to leave this world. A certain light, a halo even, would surround him. He became extra kind. His prayers turned heroic. He cried a lot. This was not always the case and maybe not all of these things happened at the same time. But they happened enough times that my martyr radar was strong; I knew when a man was finally tired and felt like he'd done his share of protecting the holy places and was ready to leave this world.

How could I go back to Tehran and order coffee on Karim-Khan Avenue after this experience? How to contemplate leaving this geography?

I slowly became, then, the keeper of the cemetery of words in this war. It was work that fell on me because these men thought one had to know something special to be able to scribble stuff down and send it as dispatches. I could live with this. It was not unlike the job of the regiment typist falling on the only dummy who took a three-week course in working a keyboard.

Nasif's news about the red house halted us. The words blanketed the room like debris after an attack. Seconds crawled by and I recalled an image of a white SUV blowing up at a checkpoint back in the Diyala Province right after Fallujah's recapture the year before. Did no one teach that militia boy never to let the driver open the passenger door, since there was a high probability it was rigged? That blast remained on loop in my dreams for the past year, and there was always the voice of someone, I don't know who, shouting *dir balak*—be careful—just before everything turned purple. And now that same purple blanketed the room with Nasif's announcement. The Afghans who had abandoned the red house, God bless them, were tired. A few of them may have been here for the love of our supreme martyr Imam Husayn, but like I said, most were strict mercenaries. Granted, they were mercenaries of the best kind, because they also believed in what they did and they'd been seasoned in the killing fields of their own country. But they would not put themselves on the line without pay. When a man takes money for his faith, he tends to get tired after a while; he wants a decent bed now and then, a warm meal, maybe a flight back to the city of Mashhad where his family are permanent refugees from Afghanistan. This is really why the red house was empty and why Nasif felt obliged to right this terrible wrong.

Grabbing his AK and taking another off a coat hook for me, Moalem cursed under his labored breath. "Professor, come! I'll take one lion over ten goat hearts."

He stomped out and I followed. Two middle-aged men with enough health problems that the last place on earth they should be was this dogfight. Just yesterday Moalem and I had finally gotten to the gist of it: our prostates. I told him that massaging mine, as the doctor had suggested, helped a little. Moalem laughed, shook his head, and told me to keep my fingers to myself, that there are different pains in the world. There was not a weapon this man couldn't handle, while I struggled even with the old reliable AK. It took Moalem a good ten minutes just to remind me the proper angle to get the magazine in. "Otherwise, even Imam Husayn can't help you!"

Mortar rounds fell near the red house. The enemy could have and should have taken a tank to the place. But their illogical conviction, much like ours, that somehow the tall red house would give them an advantage over the rest of Khan-T, kept them from completely destroying the building. When we got there, for a moment I thought that the place was crawling with them. I imagined them lurking, laughing, waiting for us to walk into their trap. The enemy, they were haters of everything, but they reserved a unique hatred for us Iranians, convinced that we personified sacrilege, the worst of the worst, Muslims who did not follow the path of the Prophet and his companions, who did not even pray properly or the requisite number of times per day. They were especially horrified at our annual self-flagellations for the martyr Imam Husayn and his family. We were idolaters at heart, they thought. Magians. Zoroastrian fire-worshippers. Off with our heads. Their loudspeakers seldom quit reminding us of our special place in hell.

A creepy silence had suddenly taken hold, as if it were just me and Moalem there while the entire town of Khan-T—sitting dumb and empty and destroyed somewhere in between the main cities of this broken country—watched us; two improbable "lions" who must take a dozen pills and eye drops between them just to be able to see and breathe from one day to the next.

At times like this irrational worries visit a man; I thought about the cell phone in my pocket and all the digital photographs on it. What if the enemy took the phone and found its pictures? I didn't say to myself: *So what! I'll be dead by then and it won't matter*. Rather than pay careful attention to our surroundings, I fixated on this useless thought. Moalem, the old pro that he was, was already clearing the red building one floor at a time. He imagined I was doing my job too, which was to hover close to a slit in the concrete and watch for enemy movement.

The photographs in my phone were an unlikely combination of portraits of Kurdish female fighters from up north and highlighted pages with scribbled notes in the margins from a torn copy of a book I had found at another ruin called Ayn al-Hosan, the Eye of the Horse, in Iraq near the Syrian border. I want to linger for a little bit on this torn-up book, or portion of a book; it summarized not the futility of our predicament here, but the way it actually gave each man his purpose, a shape to a life that otherwise would be meaningless, toiling away at hollow jobs back home. We would all die here, sooner or

later. It was what we did. I use "we" generously, however, and when I say it I don't mean myself. I mean the
fighters. They did not have to be here. Not one of them.
They came voluntarily, even if they were paid, even if
they knew Syria's bad faith would eventually send them
home—if they didn't fall into enemy hands—in a casket.

It was a book entitled *Remembrance of Things Past*. What
was it doing at the Eye of the Horse? It defied explanation. Could it have been a prank? But no: someone had
traveled from Tehran to Iraq carrying an English translation of a Frenchman's book in his pack. Why? I had an
inkling: once I'd read an American writer who said that
you can tell a true war story if you just keep on telling it.
In this war, nothing—nothing at all—made sense. People appeared and disappeared, ancient animosities suddenly boiled over, heads were cut off with such fierce
regularity that it made you doubt the proper digits of
your century, and there were so many sides and fronts
and realignments that when you managed to grab a sliver
of reliable Internet long enough to read a foreign paper, where they referred to the simple men you marched
alongside as men who committed atrocities, you began
to doubt everything, especially yourself: Am I a part of
some beastliness? Where is this inhumanity they point
to? It's not here, no. Not in Khan-T where Moalem and I
are trying to hold onto a goddamn useless red building.

I have to keep on telling this story then, like the
American writer said. A story about how, among a thousand and one other unreasonable things, I also came
across the very last segment of Marcel Proust's masterwork, near the Iraqi/Syrian border. I could tell from the
cover that it had come from a much larger tome. But

perhaps in the interest of traveling lightly the owner had cut the volume up, then taken Scotch tape to bind the cover back over the parts he was reading. The cover depicted a drawing of a woman, and what strikes me even now is that she looked a lot like the veil-less Kurdish female fighters I'd photographed up in the northwest when I'd gone there from Erbil. This synchronicity was all the more unsettling because next to many of the highlighted sentences the book owner had included bits and pieces of his own story.

But at some point this partial book had also fallen into enemy hands. I imagine they were not able to understand the English translation. Someone had written in Arabic next to the uncharacteristically undefaced woman's face on the cover, *Send to Council for research*. I could just see the Council poring carefully over Marcel Proust's baroque paragraphs, looking for enemy ciphers and hidden agendas.

After taking photos of all the pages, including the highlights and margins, I buried the book at the Eye of the Horse. I had no reason to bury it. But I did. Which gave birth to a whole series of events that came later.

Now, from my hide site at the red house, I discerned movement but could not tell if it was far away or just on the other side of the line that divided our position from theirs. The *sardar*'s voice echoed in my ear from two days earlier, telling his troops they needed to hold the line. There were so many lines here I could not tell them apart. Sometimes I thought the lines were just imaginary markers in the heads of the various sardars. Losing them would not make much of a difference and keeping them just piled on the casualties. For a moment I felt unbearably alone, in a red building that may or may not be attacked any moment, with a weapon I was not comfortable using, and a retired soldier who should be home with his family and an oxygen tank. I called to Moalem who answered immediately and came down.

I pointed down the road.

Moalem prayed under his breath and looked at me. I knew that look. *It's too late for us*, it said. There was some tenderness too to that face. A feeling of finality. It was as if we were underwater and I was hearing a voice bubbling up to say that they have a BMP and they'll probably be here in a few minutes. Moalem started to talk rapidly into the walkie-talkie, giving *gera*, positions, that I didn't understand, and before long our batteries were pounding near the BMP. The tank stopped, like an animal unsure of itself, then scurried and disappeared behind a building. But the little figures kept coming. I had long run out of disposable contact lenses for my left eye, which could see nothing without them. As a result, my right eye tired easily and would burn when it had to focus for longer than a minute. This was not going to be a heroic death; it was going to be a blind one. And I was still thinking that I didn't want the photos of the Kurdish women falling into enemy hands. They were our posters of this war, those unsullied faces carrying rifles while smiling into my camera and a thousand other cameras that had captured and beamed their images around the world. These women humored me even though they knew sooner or later they might have to fight us too, like they fought the Turks and the Syrians. They were beloved by the world. They were darlings. There was a freshness to their gazes and to their perfect suffering that was completely disarming. They were everything we were not. They were beautiful. They were angels.

A wave of nostalgia and self-pity washed over me and I started to take my phone out to erase those photographs.

Moalem shook me. "What are you doing?"

I saw my confusion mirrored in his face. *I want to delete the darlings of this war. I want to save them from the unforgiving hands of our enemy.* Moalem pushed me across the room, telling me to shoot in short bursts.

"We have to let them know someone's here and they're not coming to an empty building."

He ran to the other side and proceeded to do the same. It was a poker game and each side bluffed miserably. I started to shoot from my position, squandering shots so quickly that I muddled through two magazines. The little figures were still out there. But we'd slowed their progress. Moalem took turns shouting into his wireless while continuing to take aim. *Why had this traveler brought Marcel Proust with him to the war?* I clicked in my next-to-last magazine and started talking to myself. Moalem looked irritated with me.

"Because he thought that here, right here, he'd finally have time to read the whole damn book!" I screamed.

"What?" Moalem shouted back under the measured snap-snap of his firing.

I wished that I had at least read all the highlighted parts of the book. But I'd left that task for when I thought I'd have more leisure time. Maybe when I next went back to Tehran for a break.

Moalem now thought he saw the BMP rear its head from behind a different building. Another set of shouts into the walkie-talkie. More guns pounding the space between us.

"They are scissoring us!" Moalem yelled. It was an expression I'd heard men say countless times, and there was something satisfying about the notion of getting scissored. It had a certain finality to it. We were about to get totally cut off from our rear.

I had no more ammunition.

And so I daydreamed:

It's another one of those holy evenings in Tehran, a south side working-class neighborhood where a child-hood friend stirs enormous pots of food to give to the poor. His relative, a no-nonsense Quds commando—arguably the most-feared commando unit, besides the Israelis, in the Middle East—asks me politely not to take pictures of him, then tells me about the last time he was scissored. He recounts it with a straight face while his two little girls hover at his knees. Between the real-ization that every last man in his unit is dead and that he has run out of ammo (as I have now), and the three weeks he spent in a coma in a Moscow hospital bed, there is an entire arc of a life. This man does not live be-cause he's highly trained—if you're out of ammo you're out of ammo. He lives because he's lucky and the rest of his unit that night wasn't. Yet he still would not know what PTSD was if you sat him in a classroom and tried hammering it into him. It doesn't enter his world. It is as if he's taken an anti-PTSD vaccine that makes him impervi-ous. We both know that soon he'll be returning to the Syr-ian nightmare, but we don't talk about it. PTSD is not an option he was ever offered; it does not apply to the calculus of his life. Getting scissored for him is just another thing.

Back in Khan-T, a figure came right out into the open, and from the way he stood next to an ugly, dilapidated faux-Greek column, even I could tell he was aiming an RPG at us. I prayed that Moalem would shoot the son of a bitch already. And Moalem did—but not before the departed cleared his round. I didn't hear a blast, just the sound of something solid hitting somewhere above us and out of my field of concern. A dud? I glanced behind us and saw that Nasif had finally arrived with ten of the Afghans. They fanned out across the red building. Carrying a heavy 12.7 mm, Nasif looked me hard in my one good eye and barked, "Feed me rounds, *Ostad*, Professor!"

The dance lasted less than ten minutes. It was deafening, like always. And when it was done, all I knew was that something in our dynamic had changed. The plucky, formidable Afghans who had been guilted into coming back to their positions were kissing Moalem. Then they were doing the same to me. Meanwhile, there were three more dead bodies in no-man's-land.

The BMP retreated but survived intact.

And I, who didn't have the patience to read Marcel Proust's beautiful book, would learn in the days and weeks and months ahead to content myself with those highlighted passages. In one passage, for instance, the writer observes how some men confront death with complete indifference not because they are more courageous but because they are lacking in imagination.

Later, I'd look back on this moment at the red house as a rite of passage. Moalem had never had much imagination, and during this half-hour interval mine was also mostly—but not entirely—suspended. Otherwise,

Moalem and I would both be dead. None of the young men kissing me now had an inkling of any of this. They only knew that somehow we—two old-timers pushing middle age—saved the day by just being here. They needed to believe in our courage to believe in their own. It was an acceptable fiction.

Afterward, Moalem came up to me, smiling. "Saleh, when I finally have the good fortune to be martyred, you must take all of my notebooks. *Qabul?* You accept?" I nodded at what he thought was his generosity. What he was really doing was taking his first cautious steps toward inevitable martyrdom. He had set his feet in that vortex and there was no turning back from it.

I'd begun wearing diapers. I did not want to be in a situation in Syria where I had to piss and couldn't. Nasif, who was driving us to Damascus, had caught me with my pants down one day when I was relieving myself. It was sniper territory, with a grown man's diaper hanging in the balance. He pretended not to see it and said nothing because what is there to even say? But the whole thing made us both uncomfortable and I felt even worse for Nasif, who had to act as if there was nothing unusual happening.

In Damascus we were given plenty of rope, even though there were entire neighborhoods that remained off-limits. Two wrong turns could still be fatal. This put us on slight edge. And Nasif suggested that we go to the Zaynab shrine first, then he'd drop me off to catch a ride to Beirut. I'd first been to the Zaynab just before the war began. With a woman whose love bled us both. When she took my photograph by the citadel, I knew I was going to leave. The realization came at a moment of perfect beauty, as the Damascene sky shifted at sunset to a deeper shade of blood orange that made partings not just possible but necessary.

It was this same Damascene sky that I now glimpsed again after so long. I looked to the side of the road that lead to the Zaynab, not nearly as crowded as that first time, and saw a group of young men, Iranians, sharing some bread and cheese next to one of the shrine's many trinket stands. I knew their kind. They were me. And Nasif. They'd sold the shirts off their backs and somehow made it way out here to be Defenders of the Faith and Protectors of the Holy Places. But nobody let them into the inner sanctum of bloodletting. They didn't have the right connections with the Guards, or lacked the skills, or were just plain unlucky. They'd come here because they had nothing else going on. They came because there was something to be said about defending the faith even if, like me, you haven't much faith to begin with. I wanted to go over and kiss them. Martyrs by default, martyrs because of the poverty of their options, they were here to be immortalized as heroes. They wanted to enter the chronicles of sacrifice.

There's a passage in his book where Marcel Proust calls such men fictions in the midst of daily life.

Pointing at them, I said to Nasif, "Can't you take them to Khan-T with you?"

Without even looking their way, he dropped the Afghan accent and spoke soberly: "I don't have the authority."

"Who gave us the authority to be here in Syria? We're trespassers and you know it."

"Don't talk like that. This is war."

"That hasn't escaped me. Which is why we need the boots and the bodies."

We had become brothers of sorts, but he knew that I knew he was powerless to take those boys in. If he did, he'd have to do it for every caravan of lost souls coming here to have a go at the enemy. He didn't have the logistics for it, never mind the authority.

"I am tired of this war, Saleh. I want to go home, get married, settle down. I don't get paid nearly enough to do this. And even if I did, money isn't the reason I came here."

I was shocked. I'd thought he was counting down his days on earth.

"Why did you come then?"

He was in love.

"With an Afghan girl. I thought if I joined the Afghan units here, I'd either die, which would be a blessing, or come back a real man. Then no one would be able to deny me the woman I want."

"They would not let you marry her?"

"Worse. She got asylum and moved to Sweden with her family. Can you believe it? Sweden! I don't even know where that is. I mean, I know—but what is Sweden to me? It may as well be another planet. But you can help me. This is why I am telling you now." He reached into his pocket and handed me a small wooden prayer bead. "It belonged to my best friend, Asghar. We were together at Samarra. Please give it to his wife."

Unconvinced, I turned to him. He looked like a kid who wasn't telling the entire truth. I reminded him that he'd been in Syria for more than six months. Asghar, from what I recalled, had taken a bullet in the head at Makhoul, in Iraq, a year ago.

"Why give me this now?"

"Because I want you to go *khastegari* and ask for her hand for me."

"You want to marry the martyr's wife?"

He nodded.

"What about Sweden?"

"I don't know any Sweden."

"Why her?"

"She is my best friend's widow. It would be like marrying my brother's widow. It is the right thing."

"This logic leaves me unmoved. But all right."

"I am grateful. I am your slave."

"But what if they don't give her to you?"

"She's a widow. They might or might not. And, well, this is why I am asking you. You are honorable. They read your stories about the martyrs in the paper."

I did not bother telling him that half the outlets I'd written for over the years were long out of business and had nothing to do with martyrs.

He went on: "They know you are a friend to us. They cannot say no to your face."

"And the widow? What if she doesn't want it?"

"She wants it."

He said this turning away, embarrassed. And I knew that there was a love story here somewhere, but one so twisted that to bring it to the tip of the tongue was to commit sacrilege. This man had probably seen the widow once or twice. At most. Perhaps on leave with the martyr when they served in Iraq together. Now, in the absence of his dead friend, there was only him left and the widow.

He gave me an address in the Abdulabad District in south Tehran.

"Nasif, you are still a soldier, serving in one of the most dangerous places on earth. What if you make her a widow twice over?"

"Then she will be twice blessed."

Bullshit! None of us ever thought about how these once-, twice-, thrice-blessed mothers, wives, daughters, felt when they went down the street to buy bread in the morning. Ours was the laziest of paths, simply to die; theirs was calamity, followed by the backbreaking grind of daily life. Ours was fantasy; theirs raising that fatherless boy who'll grow up to be the spitting image of his father.

I stuffed the prayer bead, which smelled vaguely of Egyptian musk, into my pocket and punched the widow's address into my cell phone.

2

The next fortnight I spent drunk, my only contact with reality the scene from the living room window where it seemed every five minutes scavengers would dip into the large trash container in front of the synagogue, and of course the synagogue folk themselves who came every other day in their skullcaps in the early morning to take loving care of the trees and flowers of their holy place. It was probably some special time of year for them as they arrived even earlier than usual and I could hear the haunting cadence of their utterances as the sun rose above the filthy sky of Tehran with the old, grime-ridden stock exchange building in the distance. The telephone buzzed ceaselessly for the first few days but I did not have the heart to answer. The war had ruined me, and the simplest tasks were beyond me now. Washing clothes, getting food, even making tea seemed like chores that had to be negotiated in my head before being discarded. There was no agency on my part. I had gotten used to channeling daily work into rituals of prayer. The more I remained unsober, the more I prayed, believing that in this way I was staying true at least to the men I had left behind across two borders in Iraq and Syria.

Until finally one day a number flashed on the screen that couldn't be avoided: it just said *1234*.

I'll name him H, short for *Handler*. He was a heavyset man. Kind, despite his job. A man who couldn't fully wrap his will around being a state interrogator. It wasn't his style. Mostly when he called me in we'd discuss literature. He didn't understand why you couldn't put literature in the service of some greater good, like teaching young men to be more devout or more committed to the state. There was a purpose to everything in his accounting. A guy didn't write stories just for the sake of writing them; they had to strive for something bigger, more meaningful. So our "literary interrogations" ultimately had a ceiling. There was a point beyond which we could not speak to each other. And that was all right. In the grand scheme of things H was still preferable to a lot of people in Tehran. He didn't pretend to be anything other than what he was. An agent of the state. His job was to make sure you didn't stray far from certain parameters. He didn't want to have to recommend that you be blacklisted. H wasn't that kind of person. He was, ultimately, a good man. A good man in a questionable job who at least read all of my writing, and diligently. What more can a writer ask for?

"Saleh, if you go to Syria again without permission, I'll have to take away your journalist's license. Your clearance does not extend beyond Iraq."

"What's the difference? There is war in both places. In fact, it's the same war, isn't it?"

"There are rules. And rules of engagement."

My body, sore from the drinking marathon, shook involuntarily. He fished a shopping bag from a brown briefcase and then took out something from the bag and slapped it on the table. It was the Marcel Proust I'd buried in the ground at the Eye of the Horse.

"You want to explain this?"

"It's a book by a great writer."

"You've read him, this Marcel Proust?"

"Bits and pieces. Not really."

"Then who is this man named Daliri?"

"The original owner of the book, I assume. He wrote his name on the inside jacket. And those are his notes in the margins of the book."

"What's the book about?"

"I think it's about the passage of time and that we're all dying. No, that we're all dead."

"Do you not feel well?"

"I feel horrible. I haven't stopped my evil drinking since I came back. But you already know that. You know everything."

"You are a writer and a reporter. Why did you pick up a gun in Syria?"

"I hate my job. I wanted to do something that counts."

"Like shooting people?"

"Not randomly. At our enemy."

"Who is our enemy?"

"You know, the people who want to kill us."

A jolly, round-faced man with glasses knocked on the door and stuck his head inside. I'd seen him before, one of those nondescript types in a gray suit who'd probably wanted to create great works of art at one time but, out of necessity, instead ended up working at the Bureau of Censorship. H left the room to talk to him. The Proust sat like a slab of gray decayed meat on that table. It wasn't lost on me that had my interrogator been someone other than H, this book that I had buried in Iraq might be used as material evidence. For what? For anything. For being born. These things have a life of their own and when you fall into the sick orbit of suspicion by the state, anything goes. Anything. Just a thin line between farce and the utter ruination of a man. Always there. Always waiting. And so I stared at the Proust with wavering solemnity and the full breadth of my hangover and sickness.

If H would let me, I'd simply stay here, ask for a cell in the ministry to sleep in, and never leave. I needed shelter from many things.

H returned to the room and offered tea, which I accepted.

"Why did you bury the book in Iraq?"

"Someone saw me do it?"

"Of course. Someone always sees."

"You are spooking me."

"That's my job."

"Well, I knew I wasn't going to read the thing. It's just too much of a book, you know? So I took photos of where this Daliri guy had underlined certain passages, figuring those are the important parts, and then I buried it."

"Is this how one reads a book? Aren't you a disgrace as a person of letters?"

"I am. I'm a disgrace. I've known this for some time as a person of letters."

"But why bury it? Why not simply throw it away? Were you leaving it for someone to pick up?"

"This is what it's really about, isn't it? You think I left a book in English for someone to pick up. You think there are some secret codes in there?"

"No, I'm just curious at your very odd behavior."

"I didn't destroy it because it's a good book."

"How do you know? You say you didn't read it."

"One knows a good book after half a page. I didn't have the heart to just throw it away or burn it. And it was too heavy to carry around when the enemy is out there wanting to cut your head off with his constant *Allahu akbar* from a quarter klick away. So I buried it, hoping one day someone would retrieve it and appreciate its words of wisdom."

"Like what? Tell me one of its wisdoms."

"Like one character in the book talks about how war is always in a state of becoming."

"I don't understand this."

"It kind of means you can never win. No one can. War is perpetual motion. Even after it's over. You think you've won, then a few years later your win turns into a loss. Once you enter combat you've signed away anything good in this world. Men who don't understand this simple equation have a habit of turning the world to shit."

"This Marcel Proust gentleman says all that?"

"I'd like to believe he does. But I'm not so sure he actually says it. I haven't read the book, don't forget."

"Yet in Syria you join the men in the fighting instead of doing your job, which is reporting. Don't you think your behavior does not at all match what you say Mr. Marcel Proust says in his book?"

"I didn't say I'm a shining example of good behavior."

"So you admit you did wrong by going to Syria?"

"Not at all."

We went silent for a moment. He was exasperated with me, and so was I.

"Why did you do it?"

"Because there's a loss in meaning in this world and I thought I'd find it there."

"Did you?"

"Yes."

"What was it?"

"Death. It's the only thing that matters. The only constant. If you can give your death some meaning by becoming a martyr, then your death becomes significant. You will not have lived in vain."

"This is bullshit talk coming from you of all people."

"I know. But I'll take it."

I ate twenty-five miniskewers of barbecued liver. H's questioning had gone on for another three hours. He had decided to touch on all the "problematic" points of my life in one sitting. We went back over old, long-resolved territory. He wanted to know why, of all the places I could have picked to live in Tehran, I'd chosen to live across from a synagogue. Wasn't that an odd choice? And what were the chances of that even happening? It was not unlike his fixation with the Marcel Proust book, searching for significance where there wasn't any. Two years before, when I'd finally gotten around to putting together my only short story collection, he had called me in to insist I change the location of the protagonist's apartment in one of the stories.

"Why can't you change where he lives? Have him living across from a mosque if you like, or across from a shoe store or a mall or a park or a real estate office. Anywhere! Why does it have to be a synagogue?"

"Because that's where he lives."

"That's where *you* live, Saleh."

"So I'm too lazy to make up an imaginary location. Choose a location for me then."

When he saw that I really didn't care and that it was really out of laziness I'd picked my own address as the protagonist's dwelling, his mind was set at ease. But today we were back to the synagogue questions. It was a loop of pointless back and forth that one simply had to survive. His next set of questions were about Daliri, the owner of the Marcel Proust book. H wanted to know if I was aware of the guy's whereabouts.

"He is probably dead, for all I know."

H played with his fountain pen and gave me a concerned look. "What if he's not?"

He opened a drawer and took out a photograph. Daliri. Baby-faced. Beatles haircut. The look in his eyes was one of sadness or bewilderment. With some people you can't tell the difference. In a country with more opportunities than ours, he would have gotten a PhD in something precious and insubstantial. Literary theory, maybe. Or philosophy of the mind. He would have had a following of young students who swore by him and loved him. He'd marry one of them. And he'd still be sad.

Instead, what was this Daliri guy? A sound engineer for State TV in Iran. Now lost in Iraq. Or dead. Or on a boat with other refugees escaping Syria and Iraq.

All the information was in his margin notes. Our soundman for State TV had gone on location with an Iranian film crew to northern Iraq. In a battle near Sinjar he had somehow gotten separated from his team and ended up having to work his way back from behind enemy lines.

But by the time he did, it was too late; at home, they were already calling him a martyr of the war. A street was going to be named after him. All of this information he could already glean from his cell phone from across the border, while he remained invisible to friends and family. For all they knew, his phone was in enemy hands now too. They wrote to him, sent him messages which he did not answer. How could he? Providence had made an impostor of him. Now his recently widowed mother would probably get some kind of martyr's allowance. How could he go back and declare himself not dead and not a hero?

"I understand what your concern is," I said. "But I would not worry too much. If this guy were alive I would not have come across his book."

"It's not impossible there was a battle and he had to escape in a hurry again, leaving his stuff behind."

"True. These things do happen."

H gave a hard stare. "We can't have this war turn into a joke. We have to know if this guy is alive or not."

My voice faltered. "And if he is?"

"The idiots at State TV have already held ceremonies for him. There have been posters. Speeches about the courageousness of our heroic TV reporters and their teams going out there to the front lines. This guy's name makes it even more problematic: Daliri, *Courageous*. For the love of God, I can't have a man named Courageous returning to Tehran all of a sudden. We'll be a laughingstock, don't you see?"

"What am I supposed to do about it?"

"Instead of going out to Aleppo to play soldier, go back to Baghdad and start looking for this guy."

"And if I find him?"

"Tell him I better not see his mug in Iran. He has to stay in Iraq. Make a new life for himself over there. We'll give him something to tide him over for a while and we'll also help him create a new identity. We'll even give him a new name and an Iraqi passport. If he wants to get married, we'll help with the cost of the wedding. But if he comes here . . ."

"I think I get the point." After a pause, I added, "And if I don't find him? If he's dead, never to be found?"

"Then we don't have a problem."

All of this was why I was eating one skewer of liver after another. I was eating automatically, resentfully. Not because I had been tasked with finding Daliri, no. It was because once again I had encountered that wall of ridiculousness. I wanted this war to offer gravitas, but there was only more absurdity—my diapers, finding Marcel Proust at a place called the Eye of the Horse in northern Iraq, and now Daliri's fake martyrdom. I hungered for high seriousness, the way that the nineteenth-century British critic Matthew Arnold had instructed us to be serious. In fact, I'd spent a decade before this war writing essays, reviews, and criticism for local papers and journals that I imagined were serious. At the University of Art off 30th-of-Tir Boulevard, down the street from my apartment and the synagogue, where I had occasional teaching gigs, I'd tried to drill into my students the value of getting serious about things. I forced them to read in other languages, the way I'd forced myself years earlier, so that their worlds would expand beyond the stifling prison house of their native Persian with its accursed mystical poetry and Sufi drivel about transcendental love. I wanted them to break out of the petty chaos of their lives in Tehran and the endless problems of the mad Middle East and learn something about the larger world. But all of it had been an illusion; now I knew. One more war had killed all of life's buoyancy and I understood the foolishness of wanting to ever do anything—anything at all. This wasn't the first time I'd felt this way, but after achieving the near impossible in this city, which was to make half a living as a writer, I thought I'd crossed a threshold at last. The war had seemed at first like a chance to do something new, something fresh after years of borderline hack work in Tehran. That was the trouble: the war *was* fresh. It made everything else irrelevant. One became a follower, a hanger-on, an addict. I had a feeling that this Proust guy Daliri was alive, if not well, and in Iraq, unable to come back to Tehran not necessarily because he didn't want not to be a martyr, but because the war had swallowed him up—and like all the volunteers fighting there he was no longer good for anything else but playing the death game. I could not be sure about this logic 100 percent. But I thought I had pretty good insight into the man's head.

All of these considerations were not even half of the morning's interview with H. He wanted me penalized for going to Syria instead of sticking to Iraq, where my reporter's purview was.

But weren't these imaginary lines in the sand anyway? Was there really a Syria, an Iraq, a Lebanon, a Jordan?

"They are states of mind," I told him. "Ever heard of the Sykes-Picot Agreement? A midlevel British diplomat and his French counterpart decide to produce budding new countries a hundred years ago, and because of that you are telling me I can go to Iraq but not Syria? Why the hell not?"

"Because tomorrow if I see on the evening news that the enemy found one of our reporters—that would be you, by the way—and cut off his head and displayed it for the world to see, this would be, well, bad publicity for us, wouldn't it? And do you know what else? My superiors would have my job. This is why you can't go to Syria."

"On the other hand, if they cut off my head in Iraq, it's all right?"

"Don't argue with me."

"Fine, fine. I was just asking."

"Also, don't give me any more history lessons. I don't give a damn about the Sykes-Picot Agreement. Who are they? And what agreement? Forget it. I don't care."

We continued to sit there stewing in our own heads. A few years back I'd been sent to cover a film festival in a tiny West African country we were trying to have better relations with for "strategic" purposes. It was my first time back to the continent in more than a decade and I'd brought H a small African figure, the size of one of those Barbie dolls. I had to give it to him discretely because gifting your handler is bad business. But I knew I'd touched a soft place in his heart. Tears welled in his eyes and he ran his hands over the face of the African god figurine like it was a long-lost child. I knew then that both of us were wrong in our skins. Why did he have to work for the ministry, and why did I have to report about film festivals that had more prizes than entries? Our lives needed serious rearrangement, and now that I had finally tried to do something about it, he was making a big fuss.

He'd looked up all of a sudden, as if recalling something. "Do you plan to write another TV pilot?"

"They stole my last idea. State TV is filled with mediocre thieves stealing other people's work."

"All right, they stole your idea. But maybe you can do another one. This time I'll stick by you."

"Really?"

He nodded. "Write something that takes place between Baghdad and here. I'll make sure no one steals your work."

"Why didn't you do that the first time around?"

"Because you hid the pilot from me until it was too late."

"What exactly shall I write about?"

He didn't hesitate. "Write about Baghdad, circa 2006. Write about the Americans, make them as bad as you can."

"Well, they weren't exactly angels."

"Don't interrupt. Baghdad 2006. Scenario: Our guys have a few operatives in there. You'll need one main guy. A hero. In charge of . . . well, you know the rest."

"Your people need a TV series about us against the Americans? Is this why I'm here today?"

H shrugged. "Consider it a favor to me."

"If I write this, they'll give you a promotion?"

"They might."

"I'll think about it then."

"Do more than that."

3

By the time Saeed and I got to the legendary sniper he already had more kills than damn near anyone else in this war. He was a philosopher of his craft. My inadequate Arabic did not catch everything he said, but I could tell that at some point he had decided he'd had enough; he was ready to die. He had come out of retirement only because the great grand cleric in Najaf had spoken. Every able-bodied man had a duty to stand up for the country and fight the enemy. Two years later, by the time they brought him down at Hawija, the sniper's body count had become a Mesopotamian myth. I could not fathom that number of concentrated, individual kills and didn't want to think about it every time they showed him on Iraqi TV as a war hero. This war had so many impostors that when you came across a guy like Abu Abbas, you became a believer. Even the way he did the ritual wash before prayer had a sort of deliberateness that made you think of yoga and mindfulness and saintly patience. The Russians, he told Saeed and me, had been his original teachers, way back in the 1970s. He held women snipers in high regard because of their unflappability and fortitude and said that if trained properly, no man could ever match them.

I wanted him. Abbas was the unwavering rock of the

war, its cedar of Lebanon. The way he carried that SV rifle, one imagined prophets returning to speak in tongue in this godforsaken land. In Basra he admitted to us he'd never shoot a man unless he was armed, even if that man had the blood of Abbas's brothers on his hands. I believed him; I needed my champion. And when Saeed, my onetime partner, stole all the footage we had of him to make his own documentary about the war hero, I hunkered down and wrote a pilot for an action TV series based on the great man. But then, just as Saeed had stolen our collective footage of Abbas, the TV writers and producers in Tehran stole my pilot about him. Abbas was bringing me only grief. The idea of him was too good for people not to steal. He wasn't like other war heroes, people like the "Father of Death" who was a bodybuilder and a showoff. Abbas had the humility that comes with ultimate agency, that of holding the power of life or death over any man or woman at any time from long distance. He took that responsibility seriously. Which was why he hadn't trained anyone to follow in his footsteps. His takedown at Hawija had thrown my world into disarray. It was like losing a father. The enemy websites were full of celebrations of his death, and the more they celebrated the more I hated the enemy.

But I hated film people even more than I hated the enemy. Maybe it's the old envy of a poor writer who does the heavy lifting before the buzzing of the flies in the film business. First Saeed, then the O Channel from State Television. With my blueprint for Abbas's character in their hands, O Channel had gone to Saeed, bought the footage of the sniping legend, and made their stupid hit series just in time for the Persian New Year—a tired old formula of a bunch of guys with shaved heads and two-week beards walking around acting angrier than anyone should ever get if they want to live, in the middle of a war—flashing around the latest weapons instead of the shit we had to improvise with over there, and giving long, somber soliloquies about having to make "tough choices" in combat. It was bullshit pseudowarrior stuff, written by men who had seen a half year's combat at most, if that. Nothing like Abbas or others like him back in Iraq who'd been in combat nearly continuously for almost four decades.

The only poetic justice was that Saeed never finished his documentary on Abbas. He needed that one final kill recorded through Abbas's telescope lens. There's a special camera for that and while Saeed waited for its arrival, Abbas met his end at Hawija. Without that kill, there wasn't a finished product. This time, Saeed was just another documentarian waiting and, thankfully, failing at recording other people's misery.

What if I simply refused to write the TV pilot H asked for? As far as interrogators went, H was all right, but he wasn't exactly a friend, was he? The ministry could confiscate my passport and not allow me to cover another war. Then what was I supposed to do? At the paper, the *Citizen*, they'd put me in a corner of the city desk to cover small fires and stories of women who had been swindled by married Muslim Casanovas. No. I couldn't say no to H.

I waited at the Parkway fire station for Atia to come out of the *Citizen*. She always took the same route and always seemed in a hurry to squeeze into a shared taxi or a crowded Valiasr express bus before gawkers accosted her. Atia's life was one punctuated with "no"—to the bosses who wanted to sleep with her, no to the marriage proposals from colleagues at other papers and magazines, no to the lecherous interviewees, and a big no to your average unctuous fool on a Tehran street who thinks when a woman says no she's misled or playing hard to get and needs her logic set right before inevitably saying yes.

We'd been together on the ever-shuffling musical chairs of several magazine and newspaper staffs for years, always keeping that uneasy distance, not caving to the intimacy that traps folks who work on deadline in closed spaces. Readers knew her for her short biographies of famous commanders of the Iran-Iraq War, martyrs all. Capable and cool under fire, she ended up eventually running the show wherever she worked and had to play nice to the men who got depressed over her no's and the women who labored to bring her down a notch or two. She was from the northeast, and like a lot of the women of that region of Central Asia, her attractiveness was wholesome, round-faced, smiling, and crimson, and maybe that was why she got accosted so much. She was exotic in an exotic land.

"Saleh!" She held my gaze. "Why did you stop sending in reports? We heard all kinds of rumors about you. At one point, Dodonge from State TV had everyone believing you'd gone over to the enemy."

"That son of a whore would do that! Dodonge wants the Syria coverage all to himself. I ran into him near Golan, you know. There was nothing going on. But he had some Syrians start shooting in the air for effect while his boys filmed him for Channel 1. He lied right into the camera and said there was a battle in progress!"

We sat in Café Lowkey between Bahar and Mofateh. It was a small place that served the finest *kookoo sabzi* in town. The best part about the joint was that no one we knew ever went there because it was next to a mosque and had no toilet. Atia kept looking at me as if I were a brother gone awry. There had been a moment, after enough years had passed, when we considered becoming lovers. Then the moment passed because, for starters, H had called Atia in one day and read her the riot act. It was just after my "questionable" short story collection was published, when H was not sure of my loyalties. Six months later H didn't care one way or another if the two of us were lovers, because by then it had been established that the short story collection, which sold a total of sixteen copies, was hardly some foreign plot to bring down the government. Nevertheless, Atia and I had already let H's intrusion make the decision for us. It was as if his nosing into our lives was a source of assurance rather than anxiety. We didn't have to listen to him. But we did. When it really counted, we did. The things that we were not certain of, a guy like H could decide for us. He was like a holy man you go to for advice, a therapist.

"Saleh, we're not talking about Dodonge here. It's you. What's happened to you?"

"I was looking for life's meaning," I said uncertainly.

"In Syria?"

"One has to start somewhere."

One day I had watched a caravan of refugees being shifted from one place to another. There is something shameful in witnessing the hunger of an honorable woman. A mother, child held tightly to her chest, walks by not glancing at you and not asking for food, even though she's half-starved and her feet are sore and blistered. Maybe she had been a teacher in another life, a musician, a nurse, a housekeeper; she asks for nothing except that you—you who are not a part of her solution but, she suspects, a part of her misery—go away and take the soldiers you're with along with you. You are searching for life's meaning and this woman marches her misery march. What do you do? What do you file in your report? *What is it you all want from us?* she says. Says it matter-of-factly. As if reason had anything to do with why any of this was happening.

"Why don't you get married, Saleh? Settle down."

"H called me in. Told me I can't go to Syria again."

"You're not listening to me."

"I am. And I have a question for you: why don't *you* get married? Better yet, why don't we marry each other!"

"Then our mystery would disappear. Two more reporters get married to each other."

"Mystery? We're a couple of underpaid writers in a filthy, polluted city you can barely breathe in."

Atia stared at me. "Sell one of those paintings Miss Homa gave you and you'll be a millionaire. You can relax at home and think about all the literature you'll write that no one will read."

"I only have one painting from the great Miss Homa."

"Well, her sales are going through the roof, aren't they? Sit on that work one more year, sell, and get out of this business."

"Keeping my mother in a nursing home is not cheap,

you know. Even if I sell Miss Homa's painting, I'll still have to work."

"Shame on you, Saleh, for keeping your mother in a nursing home."

"Will you look after her then?"

"I can't even look after myself."

Our banter went on. In this town, writing for a living was a juggling act. You had to have seven balls in the air at all times or you'd sink. Some guys ran phony private classes for a living, scuttling from one part of town to another giving lectures on symbolism and metaphor. Others like me and Atia, we did a little of everything—a theater review here, an art review there, the biography of a martyr, a day-in-the-life of a future martyr, a film script about a sniper in Iraq—whatever it took to bring the bread to the table. One of my luckiest breaks was that the *Citizen* had needed an art reviewer when I'd needed a decent nursing home for my mother. For three years every Friday I made the rounds of the gallery openings in Tehran and would pick a couple of shows to write about. It was another side job but it gave me an in—into the moneyed class who shuttled between Dubai, London, and Tehran, fixing prices and making deals with the international auction houses. Theirs was a bulletproof way of laundering money and getting around the economic sanctions the Americans had on us. The money laundering was an art in itself; using inflated prices for contemporary art was true genius because no one could accuse you of being in the black market for frowned-upon ancient artifacts. For a penniless reporter, this mostly just meant occasional world-class food at parties where women strutted about in evening dresses that cost more than an entire combat operation at Khan-T. But it also gave one a chance to find that rare, one-in-a-thousand real artist whose cause one might champion. I'd done that with Miss Homa, who had returned the favor one day by gifting me one of her works, a medium-sized one-by-one-meter painting rendering the inside of a mosque's classic blue dome. Atia was right: Miss Homa's prices had really gone sky-high in the last couple of years and I could sell the painting.

The two of us looked up at the same moment and saw Dodonge, the reporter from the Syrian front, standing at the door of the café smiling. From the way he was smiling I knew he'd followed us here. He wanted something.

"If it isn't one of the Defenders of the Holy Places! How are you, Saleh?"

"What do you want?"

"I want you not to go to Syria anymore." He smiled at Atia as he said this.

"I was already given the message. You don't have to worry."

"Oh, I'm not worried."

"Yes you are."

As a TV reporter the man had a hundred thousand devoted fans who followed his postings religiously and treated him like a king. He was the indisputable hero of the Syrian front. Now I understood why I'd been hauled in by H for that chat. Dodonge must have been the instigator. He worried about posterity. Men like him who worked with film still had a complex about the written word. They didn't want it interfering with their carefully calibrated image. Syria belonged to Dodonge and he was here, after my interrogation, to rub it in.

Once again I realized that everything I'd suffered in the past few years was at the hands of people somehow associated with the camera, either in front of it, like Dodonge, or behind it, like Saeed. You'll never convince me that pushing a button is as hard an act as executing even a mediocre sentence, let alone a good one. But it was the Dodonges and the Saeeds of the world who received all the glory while the likes of me and Atia were lucky to get the equivalent of two good meals from a translation job that took a month's labor. This is how the world is and we suffered the malady of writers the world over: envy.

Dodonge's eyes stayed on Atia. "You should grace us too for a coffee one day, Miss Atia."

"Who's *us*?" Atia asked coldly.

"Me. Dodonge, at your service."

"Are you finished here, Mr. Dodonge?"

"Oh, and this." He dropped a small flyer on our table. "I've written a book about my war experiences. I'd like you to attend the launch. Both of you."

I was about to say that he must have hired a ghost writer, because he couldn't string together two coherent sentences on paper if his life depended on it. But Atia spoke first.

"And where will this launch of yours take place?"

Dodonge smiled. "It's a surprise. Even for you, Miss Atia."

"What do you mean, *even for me*?"

"Ah!" He smiled, nodded, and was gone.

Atia and I sat there silent. Depressed. I felt violated. Maybe Atia did too.

"Speaking of marriage," I said, "I need you to come

somewhere with me." I explained to her Nasif's situation back in Syria.

"So now you're fixing marriages for these guys? What are the chances of any of them even coming back in one piece?"

"Well, the widow will at least receive a stipend from the government."

"You are an idiot. You think this is what these women think about? They want their husbands back. They want to be a part of life, not death."

"Atia, you are the one who writes biographies of martyrs."

"It's a job."

"I rest my case."

"And no longer. The *Citizen* made me chief editor of their film section."

"No one deserves such a prestigious position more. Congratulations!"

She reached for the last of the kookoo. Our waiter was a familiar young theater actor who had dressed up like Charlie Chaplin today. Chaplin with a beard. He shuffled over, winked, and set down two teas with rock candy. "Mr. Saleh, I preferred it when you wrote art reviews. What's with writing about the Defenders of the Holy Places? I didn't take you for one of those guys."

I nodded to Chaplin. "Doesn't the Bureau of Public Places give you a hard time about looking like a homeless Westerner from a hundred years ago?"

"They don't mind Chaplin too much. I just tell them I'm practicing for a play." He smiled. "Chaplin's films were mostly silent, you know. Mute. The Bureau of Public Places likes things mute!"

Atia sucked on the rock candy as the kid walked off. I watched her. And loved her. It was an uncorrupted love, born of having fought in the same trenches, the same battles over every crumb of culture, every little weekly column we might scrounge and get past censors without having to completely sell out. I now realized that aside from the Defenders of the Holy Places, who had a habit of dying on me, I didn't really have another true friend here. Atia was it.

"Saleh, now that I'm running the film section, the boss wants you to come home from the cold and take over the art section for the *Citizen*."

"For that prostitute Mafiha?"

"You don't give him enough credit. But yes, him. Mafiha."

I looked curiously at Atia. Something was off. "Say, how is it Mafiha suddenly makes you the head of film?"

"What, you think I don't deserve it?"

"Of course you do. But men like Mafiha don't just hand one a plum. They usually have a motive."

Atia glanced away. "What if I said there was one?"

"A motive for you to run the film section and for me to head the art section of the most widely read publication in the country?"

"Yes," she said impatiently.

I didn't want to know what the motive was. And didn't care. Mafiha was the kind of guy who took and took. There was a difference between him and a man like Dodonge. Dodonge actually believed in the fight in places like Syria. He wanted to carry the fight everywhere, right to the Wailing Wall if he could, as long as he got to shine and play the hero. He was an image maker. But one who didn't mind dying for that image. I was sure in the back of his mind he was already looking forward, preparing for his martyrdom. But he wanted it to happen on his own terms and on a grand scale. Mafiha, on the other hand, was a pure wheeler-dealer; everything in his hands turned on the axis of profit. He had hounded me before to take over the art section, but not because he thought me capable as a manager, which I wasn't. But because I happened to know Miss Homa, the shining, dying star of Tehran's art world who would not give Mafiha the light of day.

"I can't do it anymore, Atia. I can't write art reviews. I never believed in them to begin with."

"You don't have to actually write them. Just run the ship as chief editor, like I do with the film section."

"I'm not like you. I'm no good at that stuff, Atia. I don't know anything about managing people."

"What are you good for then?"

I thought about the red house at Khan-T. Defending it. I hadn't been much good at that either. The whole ordeal had been an exercise in futility anyhow. The enemy had probably already retaken the place. Or pulverized it. But there hadn't been time to think about all that back then. This was what I wanted: to not think. I wanted to disappear the way that Proust guy had disappeared in Iraq.

"In any case, I have a job to do. I have to go back to Baghdad."

"Says who?"

"H."

I told her about the book and having to bury the thing at the Eye of the Horse, only to have it resurrected in front of me in H's interrogation room.

"Saleh, are you even supposed to tell me any of this?"

"Certainly not. If H finds out I told you, he'll make my decade miserable. Yours too."

"Saleh, please visit your mother."

"I will. I'll go as Charlie Chaplin. I'll put on a show at the nursing home."

Atia didn't laugh.

My mother hung on to life in such a foul mood that one of the health aides at the nursing home had called it "bad taste." It was as if Nane-Saleh only stayed put for the sake of the endless Turkish soaps she watched on television. She had never forgiven the universe for fooling her into marrying a man who did not know how to make money—my old man. She forgave the world even less for having her make that mistake a second time.

I made up for the guilt of having committed her by spending nearly every penny I made on her habitat. Five years earlier she'd buried that second husband who had squandered his own considerable inheritance and left her nothing. After that she had started going downhill herself.

As I watched her now I felt the onset of the occasional blindness in one eye that I'd experienced first back in Iraq, in Karbala. It usually became more acute when I was around death and the dying.

"Saleh, why have you come here? Go! Leave!"

"But I love you, Nane *joon*."

"You do not. You only come here to watch my suffering. Scribble, scribble—that's all you are good for! Like your wretched father. You are not a man. You are a monkey of a man. Your poverty does not interest me."

"Nane, I'm not rich, but I'm not so poor either. Look around at where you live. Not just anyone can afford this."

"Why do you have them call me Nane-Saleh? My name is not *Saleh's Mother*. You've been hanging around Arabs too long. You have become an Arab."

"Thank you."

"What do you mean, *thank you*?"

"Arabs are not like us. Their blood is warm. They mean what they say."

"No one means what they say. You are such a fool, Saleh."

"Nane! Why won't you look at me?"

"I don't want to look at you. I'm busy."

She had not been this chatty in months. It was a good sign. Unlike most mothers of the Middle East she showed her love, or those rare tiny bits of it, solely through scolding. It wasn't love to write home about, but I took it.

Her gaze never wavered from that TV. On the screen was another Turkish chef d'oeuvre with a lot of colorful Ottoman period costumes and casual overacting. I left her to her room and the make-believe. There was an ancient woman next door who wailed three times a day for exactly five minutes—as if she were calling the morning, noon, and evening prayers—warning everyone within earshot that Churchill was attacking from the south and the Bolsheviks from the north. She was living a loop of Iran and the Allied invasion of the country in 1941. It would have been funny had the place not smelled of mothballs, cleaning agents, urine, and insolent nurses.

I wish I could tell you that my heart was heavy as I

left that place. That I missed the woman who had birthed me. But what I mostly felt was an absolute resentment that included almost everyone in this city. Sleepwalkers. I would have not minded bringing the war here for just fifteen minutes—maybe up in one of the posh neighborhoods of the north side where they hired dirt-poor Afghan laborers to wipe the ground of their palatial homes where they showed off gold-plated shower heads and toilet seats. There is something about coming back to peace that makes a man rot from inside. Not every man, I am certain, feels this way, and not everyone wants to rain rockets on people who do not know, or feel, that there is a war next door.

But I felt it. Because I was rotting from inside.

Back at the house, the synagogue was jumping. There was a great big red table that had been moved out into the courtyard upon which men and women were setting plates and dishes. I thirsted for a feast like that. For happiness. For the living. The blindness in the left eye was like fireworks. There were starbursts of lights, and objects flitted about as if on holiday. I could still ride the motorcycle but it wasn't easy with just one eye. Dimensions became tricky and everybody seemed to be wearing a gigantic neon hat. With artillery shells, sometimes it looked like it was raining meteors. I would stand rooted to my spot mesmerized by my own nonseeing. Green and yellow smoke would turn into a cacophony of more color and I imagined genies of various shapes dancing on these fields of death of my own private Middle East. As men ran every which way shouting in Arabic to take cover, I stood there like a child, overcome by my ineptitude, thankful that I wasn't a soldier but a witness, a periodically blind one, free of having to grease a weapon or kick a dead enemy combatant in the ribs.

I knew I'd been tailed all the way back to the house. They'd made sure that I'd notice it too. But who could it be? H's people? No reason for it just now. Dodonge? He'd already rubbed it in by dropping in on Atia and me at the café. I'd parked the motorcycle next to a twenty-four-hour health clinic on busy Valiasr, where I knew it would be hard to steal, and caught a cab home.

The phone lit up. It was Miss Homa.

I congratulated her on her upcoming gallery show.

"Saleh, you have not come to visit my studio in some time."

"I don't write about art anymore, Miss Homa. You know that."

"That is no reason not to pay an old woman a visit."

I promised her I'd come the day after tomorrow. But even before we'd hung up, Saeed's name appeared on the screen.

I paused, hesitant to answer. In light of all that came about during this period of shuttling between peace and violence, I should have known nothing was an accident, not even Miss Homa's apparently casual call. Because the fraudulence of this calm, which I was enjoying a fragment of just then, was evenly matched by the fraudulence of the war, which sooner or later I'd have to return to.

I said a gruff hello into the phone.

Saeed cleared his throat. But I didn't give him a chance to speak.

"Listen, you human-trafficking poor excuse of a man, was it you who had me followed this afternoon?"

"Brother—"

"Don't *brother* me!"

First time we had been hitched together was in East Africa. Saeed got the job because he was a native Arabic speaker, I got it because my English was good. We were there only a few weeks together and it cemented something: we lost our minds—not completely, but enough to abandon any speck of hope we had in ourselves.

"I heard you were in Damascus," he said. "Why didn't you take me?"

"I wasn't carrying a camera. I simply went to visit the Zaynab shrine. I went for my heart."

"Your heart is satisfied now?"

I didn't answer.

"I have a job for us." He explained that a British channel needed footage and they paid well. I listened but still didn't respond. Finally, he barked, "Say something! What is your problem?"

"My problem is Africa, you son of a whore!" I hung up.

A bright early morning. We'd left the Iranian Red Crescent office to roll some film outside of a refugee camp. Another civil war. Another continent. We watched a chirpy white reporter—I don't know from where—go on a stroll for "a breath of fresh air" right under that African sky inside the refugee camp. I put away the camera and sat with my head between my hands.

A little later I'd caught Saeed working the guy, entreating him in abominable English for a foreign assignment job. When I called him a whore that first time, he looked at me quizzically and said, "Yes. Well, so?"

It was then I knew we were the living dead. Nothing mattered. Refugees. Civil wars. Atrocity. Starvation.

Someone still had to go stroll for a breath of fresh air in the madness. I went right back to the Iranian Red Crescent office to tell them I wanted out. We'd been young and adaptable back then.

Twenty years later, not so much.

But I'd found myself working with Saeed again. Because work is work. If I only relied on working at the *Citizen* and writing art reviews I'd end up in the poorhouse and my mother would have to stop watching Turkish TV.

In the meantime, Saeed could stew for a while.

The black Peugeot was still outside. Two men. They were parked near the sky-blue gate of the synagogue. The driver got out and looked directly up at my window and waved me down.

I knew him. I knew the other one who now got out of the car too. They were the State TV hacks who had stolen my idea and bought the sniper footage off Saeed.

4

Several barefoot Iraqi kids played in the mud, and in the distance the sound of big guns rumbled like an earthquake in successive waves that made one imagine beasts lurking beneath that earth.

The woman came out of her hut, unsmiling but gracious. Somebody had reported that a month earlier she'd cut the heads off two dead enemy combatants.

She offered me bread that she had freshly baked. It had been awhile since I was last in this region. The place had changed hands a few times until the men managed to push the enemy deep into the mountains beyond Tuz Khurma. Up there the sons of bitches would have to be flushed out one at a time and eliminated, and I didn't mind being a part of that operation.

"Will they pay me?" she asked.

"To film you? Yes. But you didn't keep the heads, did you?"

She looked crestfallen. "I should have kept them?"

"We must get away from here."

"But they are coming to make the film. Yes?"

"No . . . I mean yes. But they are only using you."

"What?"

She had a distant resemblance to Atia, and like Atia her cheeks flushed red when she was distraught. I wondered to myself what kind of knife she'd used in order to cut off those heads. Was it difficult? Did anyone see her do it? All we knew was that for several days the outside of her hut was decorated with them, as if it were a set for some gory medieval war film.

"Maybe," she said hopefully, "they will help me leave this evil land."

The ground shook and shook. Above us the sound barrier was being broken. Americans? A convoy advanced toward us. A last-ditch desperate battle fought by men who should have given up on this area and taken their war somewhere they could actually fight it. I saw Saeed and his British charge stick their heads out of one of the Toyotas as it zoomed past us.

The Englishman shouted, "Don't you bloody well lose her!"

I would have shouted back that he could take his cameras and his recorders and his cash and go fuck himself, but now came the inevitable: shrapnel, smoke, the earth shuddering as if a prehistoric giant had stepped on its own toes.

I stood with this woman, Zahra, who was no one's heroine. If we lived through today, Saeed would film and the Englishman would interview her, and later, if by some grace of luck she managed to leave this "evil land," she'd probably be implicated in war crimes. Someone with a degree in international law and a regular paycheck would decide that having her four brothers, husband, and three sons killed in front of her was not reason enough for Zahra to take a bit of revenge on a couple of already-dead motherfuckers.

The children who were playing next door a few minutes earlier were gone, as if they'd never existed. The convoy was gone. Saeed and his Brit were gone. It was just me and Zahra the Beheader left in this place, and I didn't even know if it was a friend or foe that was bombing us.

Nonplussed, she looked at nothing in particular and said, "I don't care if I die. But will they help me leave Iraq? Please eat the bread while it's hot. Are they your friends?"

A sharp whistle went over our heads and in the vague distance the ground did a somersault. Bread in hand and half deaf, half blind, I told her, "They are not my friends. And now we must leave."

"To where?"

"We'll start with Baghdad."

Her eyes sparkled like a child's. She repeated "Baghdad" like it was a magic charm. "In Baghdad they will film?"

"Inshallah, they will never film."

I finally lost the cell phone containing the photos of the Marcel Proust pages and the Kurdish women of combat. There would be other phones, like there would be other battles. And none of this should have mattered. Except that it did.

The outlying village we'd been trying to take was critical for cutting off the escape road from Tal Afar into Syria. The barrage of ammo that fell upon the village was senseless; it was overkill. The enemy was not fighting back because it was probably no longer there. There was no reason to lose a cell phone during a lopsided fight like this. But I did. And then I lost something far more precious.

Afterward, my days and nights turned into stirring huge pots of rice for the men in the front. I let myself go in the life of the mokeb. I did not ever want to think about another art review. I could, like a few of these guys here, hope that the war would never end. And I'd go on peeling potatoes and shouting "*moz, moz*," handing bananas to the grime-ridden, empty-eyed men who took time away from the ever-shifting front to rest awhile at the mokeb. I had already begun to fall in love with the Arabs in previous tours, but this time our struggles were the same and so my love for them turned into something acute, physical; I would have taken a bullet for any of these men. It takes time to arrive at such a place. I was willing to die for them because in the Arabs I found an innocence, a childlike bigheartedness that embarrassed my own unscrupulous world. How could men be this way and not lose the shirts off their backs? Generous to a fault, they humbled you, awed you with their transparency, and finally turned you into a better person.

One night at the mokeb, while we prepared the morning breakfast for several men of the Ali-Akbar Brigade who'd asked for the favor of billeting them for a day or two, I dug into my notebook and recalled that I'd only copied one single line from the Frenchman: *A book is a large cemetery where on most tombs one can no longer read the faded names.* Now, as I write these words, I realize that there are so many lost names to a life that the best one can do is to simplify, to not fret the act of forgetting; the soldiers in a platoon might remember every tick and oddity that one of theirs carried, but a fellow in a mokeb is lucky to remember his own name after enough time has passed, let alone the names of the dead.

One of them I'll remember, however, because the love we had was immediate—and he also happened to have the same name as the brigade we were hosting just then: Ali-Akbar.

He came in one day for tea, his hand-me-down shirt ridiculous and dangerous in its oversizedness for a crack sniper. He was rail thin and his buddies, like him, were Iranians. Volunteer dead guys. I had not spoken a word of Persian in weeks. Not even with the fighting cleric, Cleric J, who had taken me under his wing and brought me way up here to the last true front line left in Iraq. Those of us who wanted to fight on would have to move west, crossing the obsolete border back into Syria, and pretend we were still defending the holy places. We all knew it was no longer about that. It was about something else, something elemental having to do with adrenaline and revenge; I imagine hunters know something about it. We had been chased and, at times, humiliated. But now the tables had turned. Watch a man whom you've finally caught and whom you know has killed a few dozen people, mostly civilians, just because he could, because even as recently as one week ago he could afford to be judge and executioner, and because he's a piece of shit, then examine his eyes as he does not even try to protest his innocence because he knows that you *know*—see the way he goes limp inside of himself— observe him carefully while the gone-insane among you, and maybe the odd sadist, turn up to beat the soles of this man's feet before they shoot him, and you'll also know never to dishonor a man beyond a certain edge. I don't know what that edge is. And I don't want to investigate it too deeply. I just want to tell this story without the encumbrance of all the names that I have forgotten already.

Because they'll all die anyway.

I served Ali-Akbar and his three comrades—whom I'll call the Three Magi—their tea, and we spoke long into the night. They were billeted less than half a klick away with an Iraqi sniper squad, but unlike the Iraqis they had some leisure to go AWOL now and then, stay out, even mess around with their ammo, leave stuff behind that the normal army structure would have chewed them alive for. Who else could do this but the Iranians who didn't have to be here but came anyway, in order to "help" their brothers? So the Iranians were humored. The locals were grateful. Even at the mokeb they treated someone like me differently. "Saleh, do you seriously enjoy getting shot at? Go back to Tehran. It's heaven there."

I didn't want heaven. Heaven is a bore.

And confounding.

5

Ten days after the interrogation with H, I'd finally traveled to south Tehran to arrange that marriage for Nasif who, I assumed, was still fighting in Syria.

And I'd taken Atia along with me.

"Are you taking my family for fools?"

The father of the young widow/bride-to-be had said this immediately and my heart sank even before he'd finished. I looked at Atia, who looked away. By now martyrdom was a way of life. It was the grammar of our everyday lives, not just an appendage to it. In other words, I knew the news of another death was on someone's lips even before the news had been spoken.

Atia pressed for the sake of appearances, "*Haji Aga,* our intention is pure." She said something about Nasif which I didn't catch. I was waiting for the bad news to drop and . . . then it did.

The bride-to-be's father set his phone between us, tapped the app that most of the fighters I knew subscribed to, scrolled down to the latest news from Syria, and there it was—the news of Nasif's martyrdom.

"When?" I asked.

"Yesterday."

I took the cell phone and scrolled through more photos. Blood-soaked posts and also romantic ones. All of them filled with the claptrap of an "honorable death." War had turned into a game of telephone tag. What was happening to us? It wasn't just Nasif who'd died. They'd all died. Moalem was dead. So were several of the Afghans. Khan-T hadn't fallen, but the red house finally had—a place no one should have fought over in the first place.

You can tell a true war story if you just keep on telling it.

Sensing my disorientation as we stepped out of there, Atia guided me to a smoothie shop nearby. I had been thinking of that opening sentence from the famous Hemingway story: *In the fall the war was always there, but we did not go to it anymore.* The line kept echoing like a song I'd sooner forget.

Yes, the war was always there, but in fact it always came at us; we couldn't avoid it. And it wasn't just one war; it was wars, one blending into the next like an ill canvas. The war never ended.

Atia said, "It's as good a time as any to tell you something."

My heart sank for the second time that hour. "What?"

"Remember that talk we had about marriage? I've decided to do it. Get married."

"I'm in mourning, Atia. Do you have to tell me this now?"

"It's precisely the right time to tell you. We just went to that house to ask for a girl's hand in marriage. Her husband's dead. So is her new suitor. Remember that Hebrew poem you once translated but the Censorship Department wouldn't allow you to publish?"

"Atia, for the love of Imam Husayn! Now is not the time to have a literary discussion."

"That poem said Ecclesiastes was wrong to tell us we don't have time for everything. We do. We do! Because it's the only life we get, Saleh. We most certainly do have seasons enough for every purpose."

"What are you talking about?"

"I hadn't told you, but our dear boss, Mafiha, has been proposing to me for six months now. I've finally decided to say yes."

It was a punch in the gut, coming right after the news of the death of my men in Syria.

"So this is what you've been doing while I've been away? Flirting with the chief?"

"Saleh, I'm not some teenager. Don't speak to me that way. I'm your colleague. And friend. And what this is, is not flirting. It's called life. And change."

"But . . . with Mafiha? That fraud?" I barely managed to get the words out.

"He's not a fraud. He simply takes his opportunities."

"If you say so."

"And he's not such a bad writer."

"You mean all that peace-poetry shit he's been publishing lately?"

"Peace is not a bad thing, even if some people take advantage of it."

"My sentiments exactly."

"Come on, Saleh. Give me your blessing. I beg you. Besides, like I told you before, Mafiha wants you to edit the art section at the paper."

"With Imam Husayn as my witness, I'll do no such thing."

"All right. How about just giving me your blessing then?"

"What, bless you for marrying a guy who deals with art like it's real estate? What about truth? What about all the men I knew who just got mowed down in Syria?"

"That is exactly what I mean. What about them?"

"They're dead!" I shouted. "But Mafiha, your boss and I guess husband, isn't. Dodonge, the apparent fucking prince of the Syrian front, isn't. And that other whore's son, my so-called partner, Saeed the fake documentarian, isn't either. Men die while these motherfuckers take their books and photos and films on tour to Europe and win awards for them. Something stinks about all this, Atia. The world fucking stinks."

"Something does stink, you're right about that. And that's your self-righteous nagging. You think I don't know what you're up to?"

"What am I up to, Atia?"

"You're no better than Dodonge or Saeed or, if you will, Mafiha, my husband-to-be. You want to manufacture glory for yourself off of dead soldiers' backs. At least a guy like Mafiha just writes a few poems. And he's a first-rate editor. Without him none of us would have jobs. But what about you? I've read your reports from over there. We all have. You make it sound like you're under attack 24/7."

"In war you're always under attack. Even when you're not."

"Don't give me your philosophical bullshit, Saleh. I know you better." She paused for a second, added a "Fuck you," and then burst into tears.

"For the love of Imam Husayn . . . Atia *jaan*, take it easy. All right, I accept."

She said softly, "I'm tired of this running, Saleh. I

want to write my books. I want to not have to wake up every morning thinking how I'll make next month's rent."

"But why him? Are the men in Tehran such shits that you had to settle on *him*?"

"Yes, they're shits. He's just a little bit less of a shit, if you will. And a winner."

I sighed. "That he is."

"And he's not dishonest in love, Saleh."

I winced. "Fine. I get it. Don't go there, please."

"And he wants you back writing for us too, even if you won't edit the section. Imagine, when I'm Mrs. Mafiha I'll look out for you 100 percent. You'll get a raise. I'll have them send you on sweet foreign assignments, not ones where you get shot at." She meant all of this and she'd stopped crying. She was like the mother I'd always wanted. She repeated, "Bless me, Saleh. Please!"

"But if it's only a matter of marriage, *I'll* marry you. Yes, why not! I'm proposing right now."

She looked away, exasperated. "You're an idiot, Saleh."

"Why am I an idiot?"

"Because you are consumed with martyrs and martyrdom, while Mafiha wants to live and let live."

I muttered, "Sort of like you, I suppose. You're pretty good at this business of living too."

"Yes," she hissed. "And why not? Why can't I be good at life?"

"With Mafiha as your life partner?"

"Yes, with him. Why not?"

I said meekly, "But Atia, those peace poems he writes!"

"Shut up, Saleh! He's more than just those poems. He's a good guy. He sticks around. He's capable. That counts for a lot."

"Some would call what you're doing selling out."

"Or buying in."

"Aren't they the same thing?"

"They're not. And if you had half the brains he has, you wouldn't let people steal your documentary footage or your TV pilot. At least at the paper, I can watch over you. You're a child, Saleh."

It's not a good feeling getting deconstructed like that. She couldn't have possibly meant it when she said I was as awful as Dodonge or Saeed, could she? Suddenly my whole existence was in question. The men in Syria were dead. Men who had saved my life more than once. Gone up in smoke just like that, and I didn't even know how. Maybe I was a pimp in this war, after all. It was sickening.

I reached out and barely brushed Atia's hand.

She looked back at me. Sad. Exhausted. Thoughtful. "Bless me, Saleh. Bless me, I beg you."

And I did. I blessed her marriage in the Abdulabad District of Tehran, at a smoothie shop across the street from the home of the widow who might have been another young man's wife if it hadn't been for a miserable, utterly purposeless piece-of-shit red house in faraway Syria.

6

Yet it was the sniper Ali-Akbar's accidental martyrdom in Iraq, and not the martyrdom of the men in Syria, that finally sent me into a tailspin. I had stopped sending dispatches from the Eye of the Horse. And after my phone was lost in that truckful of onions while we were preparing to liberate the village outside of Tal Afar, I was at last free from having to answer to anyone about anything. H couldn't find me unless he sent Military Intelligence way out here for someone they could care less about. H, I knew, hated Military Intelligence as much as they hated ordinary Intel. Besides, they had more important things to do than play cat and mouse with a stray, half-committed journalist.

The Americans were firm about us not going anywhere near Mosul. Behind the scenes, it was their play in that direction, and we let them. That city was going to be a goddamn dogfight anyway, and the Iraqi regulars could take the brunt. We stood to the west, by Syria, and bided our time, continuing to choke the escape routes out of Tal Afar, killing when we had to and feeding the hungry when we could. We'd meet every afternoon at Khaled's place across from my mokeb and trade war gossip. That day I was serving tea in front of the mokeb at twilight while a herd of sheep scampered by, bleating with an irritated persistence which made you think they too were sick of it all and would sooner be eaten. Khaled came over. He smoked like a man possessed. And at that moment he was. A Turkmen out of Mosul who had lost everything to the enemy, he spent his days perusing military-grade Western satellite apps that you had to pay a small fortune to get and have security clearance for but which all of us in Iraq had for free because someone somewhere had cracked the code. Someone always cracks the code. Khaled would show me the very window to his house in Mosul, or what was left of it, and peer at the cracked screen of his cell phone with the hunger of a man who does not necessarily want revenge but simply to rebuild again. Nothing replaces home and no one exemplified its absence more than Khaled, who now gave me the most concerned look in all of Iraq just then (which is saying something), when he asked: "*Weyn* Ali-Akbar?"

"He'll show up. Don't worry."

I watched him go at his cigarette like he might swallow the thing. Like a man who had survived a death patrol. I've only seen combat soldiers smoke this way. Them, and hopeless, beyond-the-pale drug addicts.

"But he is always at my place this time of day."

"Maybe he got held up at the *sater*, in the trench."

"He always lets me know."

Khaled paced around the tea stand. A convoy of heavy guns thundered by, making the petulant sheep run every which way. Haji Yusuf, our septuagenarian inspiration, held up his AK inside the mokeb and let out a few rounds in honor of the convoy, his white hair dancing to the dust as Cleric J came hobbling out of his quar-

ter without his one prosthetic leg and gave Haji Yusuf
an earful for acting childishly inside a bustling mokeb.
This, of course, only buoyed Haji Yusuf, and so he let
out another spray of bullets and danced his southern
Iraq tribal dance to the good cheer of the soldiers—he
was a man from Kut, where the British had suffered their
most humiliating defeat of WWI in the Turkish theater
of war. This slight detail somehow seemed significant to
me, though I wasn't sure why.

Khaled smoked.

Then I felt cold sweat on my palms. The sky over
northern Iraq just then was as holy as I'd seen above Damascus while saying my last goodbye. It was an orange
to give your life for. And that's what men did: they gave
their lives for it.

Khaled said, "Let's go to their billet and find out."

We went. Ali-Akbar's Iranian mates, the Three Magi,
weren't there. A young Iraqi sniper, all of sixteen, pointed
to a white Toyota with two men inside. Iranians. Intel
men. One could distinguish them from regular soldiers
by their jadedness and general lack of enthusiasm.

Khaled asked the question—where was Ali-Akbar?

There are some words you never want to hear if you
can help it. Yet after you hear the word, you just have
to rearrange your brain and tap deep into your drying
well of stoicism or else you'll lose your mind: "*Istashada*.
Martyred."

The mokeb became my Ferris wheel. Cleric J and his
team had done their stint for the month and were
ready to head back south to their wives and children.
It was night and we lay in a filthy room the enemy had

booby-trapped four previous times. The only thing that never changed about the room was the framed picture of some old European fairy-tale gingerbread house on the pock-marked wall; no matter how many times this place switched hands, neither side took the framed picture down to smash it to pieces. I could not figure it out. Maybe in the hearts of all of us, a light burned for Hansel and Gretel and cease-fires.

And probably this had been the room of a child once.

Outside that room was even filthier, the mokeb a monstrous trash heap with the drying and despicable turds of good-natured, often lazy men who seldom bothered to take their business elsewhere.

On more than one occasion I'd watched Cleric J turn combat into a dance. His business was faith and supply lines. In war he turned into a kid in a candy shop. Saeed and I had discovered him when the war first began. Somehow he always got himself into the thick of the fray. And there he stayed, directing bumbling tank traffic as if he were General Rommel, and killing time in no-man's-land so that enemy snipers could casually take a crack at him. I didn't understand him, but I loved him. He was also useful. I could hide behind his clerical robe and avoid Iranian Intel who'd sooner shoo me home and back to writing pointless art reviews.

"Saleh, if you stay here too long you will become like me. War will get into your skin and bones and you will forget your duties."

Cleric J's Persian was singsong. He had spent most of the years of Saddam's dictatorship in Iran and learned our language. After losing three brothers and a leg he was still fighting. The boyish good nature in his voice didn't let up even when men were trying to stuff their oozing guts back into their split bellies. I wondered if he'd ever had nightmares. Whenever he quoted from the Koran a mischievous twinkle came into his eyes, as if to say, *I really do know this stuff and I am firm in my faith, but it's not where my heart is. My heart lies with the men at the sater.*

"What are my duties then?" I asked.

"You don't have a wife? I'll get you one in Diyala. Come back with me. Take a rest. We'll come back here in three weeks. Don't worry!"

"I can't leave here for three weeks."

"You have the bug of *nabard*, the thirst for combat. I can tell."

"And Intel will force me to go home if I head back south with you."

"They won't. They came to see me. I told them that this man—you—has lost his mind. But in proper fashion. He desires martyrdom. And that you—meaning *they*—cannot deny you—meaning *you*—this."

"What did they say?"

"Nothing. They went home. Or wherever it is those kinds of men go to at night."

"So you'll let me stay?"

"The mokeb is yours if you wish to stay. But you must not do it for the wrong reasons. If it's martyrdom you seek, I am with you. But if you want to just stay here and mourn your friend Ali-Akbar, then you are acting spoiled and also dishonoring your friend's perfectly adequate martyrdom, and so you must return to Diyala with me to find you a suitable wife."

"I will, inshallah, see you in three weeks, *ya sayedina*."

* * *

There was never time to mourn. The mokeb was always replenishing itself. Other mokeb crews came and went while Cleric J and his men were on leave. They came equipped to be generous, men who had fought at other times in the same places but now kept to the background and took pleasure in the art of feeding warriors. At night, as my eyesight went from bad to worse, we'd sit in the long room and trade stories. The Arabic was viscous with all the head-splitting variations of Mesopotamia, and after a while instead of better understanding what was said I withdrew into my near blindness and added deafness to the mix and kept stirring the rice, unfreezing the chicken, and chopping the onions. Without a cell phone for the time being, I was a man tethered only to God's will.

Before long, Khaled took the heavy truck and went to join the government forces gathering outside Mosul. I could not blame him. Mosul was his home. The waiting here was like cultivating mold, and after Ali-Akbar's premature death even martyrdom seemed questionable, though we never mentioned it. Then a man in charge of intelligence for the formidable Kataeb forces came up from Baghdad and ordered the rest of the Iranian sniper team, the Three Magi, to go south with him and then home. One dead Persian from a sniper squad was enough to put him through the ringer. He didn't want more. This left me alone to my sealed-in circumstances. I smiled a lot at my revolving door of Iraqis who were especially enamored of this thing called Facebook and who watched me wide-eyed when I explained I did not yet have an account. Who knows if years from now the name will even ring a bell, but back then, in that geography, this virtual republic of Facebook was the river that connected the Arab warriors. They took pictures of themselves five minutes before dying. Then, three minutes before dying—if luck and bandwidth were with them—their smile was making the rounds on the Internet, immortalizing them just as they were about to leave the world. It was an odd, even batshit-crazy metastatement on the last thing that might be thought sacred: combat. We should have already known nothing was sacred. We were simulations. In another year or two tourists would probably be roaming this very ground where Ali-Akbar had stepped, stupidly, on a trip wire inside a school building while we took that village.

We were, in other words, ornaments.

In the meantime, I kept trying to wrap my mind around that day of Ali-Akbar's loss. Cleric J had been pushing the men forward toward the village with his "God is great" bravado while I stood back, camera in hand, marveling at his brilliant madness. Some Arab guy was doing a little victory dance with the AK raised over his head even before the village was fully secured. I didn't know where Ali-Akbar and the Three Magi were. I imagined, being snipers, that they were far from the main action. Taking aim. Sealing escape paths. Cutting down stragglers. A half hour later, after I'd shoved a banana to each victorious brother, a dozen guys came out from the schoolhouse repeating the Koran verse, "To God we belong and to him we'll return." They carried a blanket from which only a leg stuck out. I'd trained the lens on that leg, Ali-Akbar's leg, not realizing that that was him with a missing head and arms.

"Hu istashada. He's martyred."

It wasn't as if there hadn't been others. The martyrs in Syria, for starters. But somehow this was the one that really did me in. And Khaled too. To get taken down because you trip over a wire in a schoolhouse! What was he doing there in the first place? It was too close to the action. In fact, the schoolhouse *was* the action, and no sniper motherfucker should have been there. But he was. And therein lay the issue. Ali-Akbar was the war in all its stupidity. He'd left home, crossed the border, and come here for *this*?

I thought of that Hemingway saying again but tweaked it a little: *In the fall peace was always near, but we did not go to it.*

Then one day Saeed showed up at the mokeb. Alone.

Cleric J and his people were due back in a couple of days, but rumor had it that the enemy was planning a second reckless attack on the town. A week earlier they'd made a beeline for the center, which was us, because across the street behind where Khaled's quarters had been there was a fuel depot. The fact that they didn't blow it up, which would have been easy, but instead tried to take it over and escape with the fuel, showed desperation. The noose continued to tighten in the west, and to get to Syria they'd need that liquid which they were running out of. Their suicide mission made this obvious, which also told us all we had to do was hold ground.

We almost didn't. There had been men with absurd, Akkadian-length beards shooting in broad daylight and strutting down the dusty thoroughfare, as if this was Main Avenue on a Friday afternoon, before they were finally brought down. I'd lain low inside the mokeb and mostly seen two of everything with my bad eye until the crisis was over.

A week later my eyes had settled a bit, and when Saeed came at me in the mokeb I saw, correctly, only one of him, and there was no mistaking what he was about to do. His first swing missed, and before he had time for a second swing four burly Iraqi men had him by the arms and wrestled him to the ground. He was screaming in Arabic, telling them to let go and that there was a score to settle.

I took him to the room with the gingerbread house on the wall. "I've done nothing to you. Why do you come to my mokeb and embarrass me?"

"There's a war going on, in case you've forgotten."

"I haven't forgotten. And every man out there has a weapon and this is my mokeb."

"Yours?" He laughed.

"What is it you want?

"I lost the contract with the British station. Because of you. You disappeared on me in Tuz Khurma and took that head-chopper woman with you. Where? I have no idea."

"There are ten thousand stories in every little town in Iraq right now. They need to have the one about a woman who cut off a couple of heads that were already beginning to stink?"

"That's what makes the story. It's why the English guy wanted it. It wasn't your business to make that call."

"But I did."

"Where is she?"

"I took her away so a whore's son like you—and your

masters—won't make a caricature of her for foreign TV. She cut off those heads because she was angry. I can understand that."

"You can?"

I said nothing. I didn't understand anything. I'd set up Zahra the Beheader in the sprawling Sadr City quarter in Baghdad for the time being. She'd become my charge because everything I'd suffered at the hands of TV bastards like Saeed came down to keeping her from them.

"Go out of here. Please!"

"What, you think you found your calling making lunch for the militias?"

"And dinner." After a while I added, "And breakfast."

"Please, Saleh! I can't work in Iraq without someone who can speak your kind of English. All right, forget about the head-chopper. Get your backpack on, we'll go to Baghdad and find new work with some other Europeans."

"Fuck the Europeans."

"Why?"

"Because this is their mess." I mumbled, "Sykes and fucking Picot."

"Say what?"

"Nothing. Just go away."

There was an AK hanging off the wall and like a fool he jumped, grabbed it, and aimed it at me. "I'm taking you to Tehran then. For disappearing like you did, they'll send you to that place where grown men have to beg for their mothers."

"Put that thing away, for the love of Imam Husayn."

He put the weapon back and sighed. I could tell he felt silly.

"Listen, Saleh, the audience for the *Abbas: Sniper Legend and Fist of God* serial has shrunk to half what it was two months ago. Do you understand what that means back in Tehran? O Channel is blaming you for it."

"I'm not responsible if their writers can't write. They should have thought things through before they bought the film footage from you. Footage that, by the way, you stole from me."

"From us. I stole from us. There's a difference."

"Well, at least you admit to the theft."

His face turned morose and sulky. "You made a deal with O Channel before coming back out here. You're going to write for them again. I've heard about it."

"I could not exactly refuse."

It was the day they'd followed me from my mother's nursing home. By then they were already stuck for new ideas for the *Abbas* show. I'd asked them why they didn't just wrap it all up. The show had already completed its arc and now it was time to wind it down. But word from the ministry was that the series must go on another year. Their exact words: *The restive population, nervous about the state of the currency against the dollar, needs an antidote to keep it home watching programs that promote both patriotism and partnership with our good neighbors.* In this case, the "good neighbors" were the Iraqis. It was also why H had insisted I come up with a new pilot that followed a hero circa 2006, when the Americans were deep in Iraq. I had said yes to both, since saying no was not an option, and then I had disappeared back into the maw of the war here.

I did not see a healthy return to Tehran and Saeed knew this.

A commotion had broken out outside. Men were

shouting. Someone was popping off AK rounds and for a moment I thought Cleric J might be back and that was old Abu Yusuf being overenthusiastic with his weapon, as usual. But the scene in the open area of the mokeb looked positively violent. More people came inside to see what was going on, where a tight but widening circle of men were kicking and swearing at something or someone. I could not catch what they were saying.

A teenager from Najaf who'd been helping at the mokeb ran toward me. "Come! *Ta'aal, ta'aal!*"

People made way. On the ground I saw the pummeled, bloodied face of a young man. Maybe nineteen. You could see his beard was choppy, like he had been trying to cut it with a knife in a hurry. He looked half-starved and ready to fall asleep or die. The kicking barely made a dent in him. He was done. He had the long, handsome face of a North African, and when I was told he might be Tunisian I wasn't surprised. A van screeched to a halt outside the mokeb and two men came running toward us.

"He's ours. We'll take him."

No one gave way. One of the kitchen guys shouted back, "He's not yours! We found him hiding in the mokeb. He's ours. Who are you?"

They tried pushing past the crowd but were shoved back. It was a standoff to see who owned the enemy combatant. He'd probably been cowering in some dark corner of the mokeb ever since last week's misbegotten blitz on the town and somebody going to take a dump in private had finally found him. The two men, from whatever outfit they were, really didn't have a leg to stand on here. We weren't part of anyone's command structure.

We didn't have to give up the kid if we didn't want to. What I didn't know then (and I should have) was *why* we weren't giving him up. I realized that with those two men he had no chance, wherever they took him; what I didn't realize was that he had even less of a chance with us.

"It is up to you!"

I turned around and saw the Najafi kid, his unlikely curly blond hair caked with the dust of northern Iraq and Syria, whispering in my ear. "You are Cleric J's man while he's gone. Whatever you say goes here."

The kid's whispering suddenly turned all attention our way. The Tunisian remained on the ground, coughing weakly. "*Ma*," he whimpered.

I gestured to the Najafi kid, who picked up one of those ubiquitous bottles of water for the fighters from right by his foot and took it over to the boy. I was not sure, but it felt as if we were slowly being sucked into some evil. Nearly all the men in that mokeb had had some kind of history with the Iranians going back to the Saddam days; it was a factor that carried cachet. And to be Cleric J's rep carried even more. As I started toward the two men, I noticed that Saeed was at the periphery of the circle, camera in hand, filming. When you spend enough time with a group of men, even if it's through the revolving door of a mokeb, when you feed them for days on end and call them heroes even if you only half mean it, when you give them aspirin (because that's all you have) even though it's voices they're hearing inside their heads and they thank you anyway like you've given them the last elixir on earth, something happens between you and them—call it a bond, a special contract of blood that an outsider best not meddle with.

One frown in Saeed's direction was enough for the four burly men who had held him down before to do it again. The mokeb seemed to be in a time warp, everything slowing down—the North African on the ground, starved and eminently executable; the two men who had materialized out of nowhere looking annoyed and confused; and Saeed pinned like that, his camera thrown to the side, its lens open and layered with fresh dust.

"I'll get you for this, Saleh."

It was the last thing Saeed said as they manhandled him out of the mokeb and away from the Eye of the Horse.

The boy was killed two days later.

I went blind for six hours with the news. Afterward, I drank in the miracle of vision like it was my first time seeing. Even the sight of mounds of discarded plastic bottles was like witnessing a wedding. I forgot that North African boy we killed because he was guilty and because we could. Someone had to do it, and the guilt only stayed as long as I had time to dwell on it in darkness. When light returned to my eyes, the boy was history. I did not give a fuck about his fate. Well, maybe I did. But tangentially. Maybe it was he who had set the trip wire that killed Ali-Akbar. I doubted it. But I did not dismiss it either. It was easier this way; it allowed me to live with us. Maybe the world was right and we were beasts after all. But what did the world know? Where was the world anyway, and what did it have to do with the Eye of the Horse?

I wanted to go to Baghdad and have a few shots of hard liquor. Anything would do. Then I would pick up

Zahra the Beheader and take her with me to Tehran to give her new life. All she had done was the thing many of us would if we had the heart. I still see that North African boy lying on the ground of our mokeb. I tell the men to throw him in a room and tie him up. Cleric J will be back in a day or two and he'll decide. But by morning the night shift had already gone to work on the kid and even filmed him, because this war, all of it, was on video. He admitted to having killed many of us. In combat and through executions of civilians. You name it, he'd done it. He admitted it all methodically, as if he were counting off from his grandfather's abacus. I despised him for his truthfulness. He left zero room for mercy. Perhaps he thought that since lying would get him nowhere, which it wouldn't, telling the truth to its last detail might. Where did he think he was? He was inside a mokeb of the Hashd forces; we did not forget, period.

The next afternoon Cleric J was back and handed me a Colt. "Saleh, he's your charge. Do it! The men expect no less."

"If I don't?"

"This war is not a holiday, you know! You are not on vacation."

He wasn't angry with me. He had said it casually, matter-of-factly.

Twelve hours later, when we were serving tea at dawn to the first replacement convoys of the day heading for the sater, I saw that old Haji Yusuf was grinning.

"Your man went swimming late last night. He's not coming back."

"The North African?"

"Him."

"Who carried it out?"

All of a sudden Haji Yusuf had never looked so sober. He might have been one of Lawrence of Arabia's boon companions, laying charges on the railroad tracks of this land circa 1916 and singing ancient poems of the desert deep into the night.

A century had passed. Yet not a lot was different in this landscape. We were still fighting the same fight.

"I have had six sons and forty-two grandchildren and great-grandchildren. Out of those, I have lost two sons and two grandsons to two wars. So I thank you."

"Thank me for what?"

"My satisfaction."

It would not do to hang around for much longer. I had thought the end was close. But the enemy thought otherwise. They had nothing to lose now, so they fought like rabid dogs. Sometimes we'd find them dead, chained and locked to their weapons. Men speak of grudging respect for a capable enemy. I had none of that. Rather, I was irritated by their pluck and didn't want to share my God with theirs. They needed to find another alphabet and say God's name differently than us. Which was why whenever we smoked them out of their lairs and captured their black flag with Allah's name on it, the first thing we did was to turn the flag upside down and take a picture. It was the ultimate insult, this. God's name was turned on its head and it was no longer God but something else. Something foreign and unworthy of attention because it had been manufactured by men who knew neither God nor His Prophet.

Nevertheless, by being as dogged as they were, they

stole the show. We wanted them to just go die some-where. But they had other ideas. And when my left eye started to really go bad, as bad as some of the gassed vets I'd seen with their permanently damaged corneas, I decided to go home for a respite. I had done nothing for Tehran and their expectations. Losing the cell phone had been a master stroke—it absolved me of having to look for the Proust guy. Though this meant that H would be waiting. And so would the O Channel thugs.

Peace, ultimately, was a problematic condition.

War, putting everything on hold, was sometimes more desirable.

I went back to Baghdad to fly to Tehran. But I did not go to Sadr City to fetch Zahra the Beheader that first night. Instead I took a hotel in the Karada District and went to my usual corner liquor joint off Abu Nuwas for a bottle. It was obviously bootleg Scotch and tasted du-bious but it did the job. Next day, wracked with both a hangover and guilt, I called my friend Jasim who imme-diately began to berate me.

"Do you know how many calls I got from Tehran from people looking for you?"

"I can guess."

"What is this number you are calling from?"

"I lost my phone. I'm in a hotel." I gave him the place's name.

"Don't move from there!"

I did.

Jasim worked for a TV network in Baghdad loosely connected to the Hashd forces. He was the kind of man of whom you think: *if there were another ten thousand more of him, this country would not be in such a state of putrefaction.* In-

stead, he did fixing and producing jobs for next to nothing for inept people who had dollars, people who'd never
know Jasim was saving their lives at least five times a
day in the Baghdad of now, just as he had done in the
Baghdad of ten years earlier. He was the quintessential
guy behind the scenes, quietly smoothing the way, loved
by even the worst of men because he stayed honest to
his own disadvantage. I always had the feeling that if Jasim too one day went up in smoke in a suicide bombing,
then I wouldn't want to live anymore. It wasn't because I
loved him, which I did, but because there comes a place
where you have to draw the line with God. Not everyone should have to die. Somebody should stay around,
somebody without bloody hands.

But I couldn't face Jasim just now. He was too responsible a citizen for me to face with a hangover. I'd
left Zahra the Beheader in Baghdad to live temporarily at
Jasim's house with his wife and two children. But Sadr
City was a sprawling meganeighborhood of love and
dashed hopes, where extended families put on slippers
and shuffled from house to house to visit next of kin,
and next of next of kin, for hours on end every night
when the weather cooled down. How would Zahra the
Beheader, who had lost everything and had been on the
verge of being put on display like a circus freak, get by
in Sadr? I didn't know.

I ran out of the hotel toward the long-suffering wa-
ters of the Tigris at Abu Nuwas. Down the road there
was a checkpoint. Young men stood by the river laughing, as if the war was a million miles away. You couldn't
begrudge them that. The war was right here at that
sleepy checkpoint. We all knew it and still acted like a

checkpoint made a difference. I did not know why I had even bothered to let that North African enemy boy at the mokeb get a drink of water. Wouldn't it have been better to not give him hope?

"You really need to get yourself a wife, Saleh."

Jasim, smallish and prompt and neatly dressed in his standard gray suit, stood next to a palm, eyeing me with some concern. Being the professional fixer that he was, I knew his MO. He'd called the hotel desk and told them to have the Iranian followed if he left the hotel. Jasim's true job was to survive. Once, two American rockets had fallen on either side of him by the Eastern Gate souk. He should not have survived and had the right to wax philosophical about it ever afterward. But platitudes were not his thing; he never said things like, *Every day above ground is a good day.* He knew better than to think this bullshit was true. Many days above ground are worse than death.

A magnificent pile of garbage floated twenty meters away from us on the river, the sun shining off it as if it were jewels and not more plastic.

"For the life of me, Jasim, I was ready to marry two months ago. But she went and married a so-called poet."

"A good poet?"

"As fake as they come. He writes antiwar noise and reads in famous world capitals. They get translated and he gets invitations to talk about peace in our time."

"Why don't you do the same?"

"I would if I believed in it."

"Then there is no hope for you."

"Besides, this poet is also, kind of, my boss. In other words, the woman I would have married went and married the man who signs off on my paychecks."

Jasim said nothing. Something was wrong. Usually he had a lot more energy than this. He didn't deal in pessimism and hopelessness. Not even with rockets dropping on him at the Eastern Gate. On the phone he'd been just about ready to kill me, now he was subdued. He had something to say.

He sang in the loveliest Arabic that a man can sing: "*The greatest loves relinquish all hope of union.*" Then he laughed, bitterly. "Listen to me! Am I quoting the great al-Mutanabbi or the great Ibn Zaydun or only my humble self on a street named after the great Abu Nuwas? And this while you speak of fake poets. What was the name of your love?"

I said Atia's name.

"Saleh, something has happened!"

I took a breath. I had an idea what was coming. "You wish to tell me something about the woman from Tuz Khurma. Yes?"

He nodded.

"Dead?"

He nodded again.

"How?"

"She got it into her head she wanted the world to know her story."

"She told people what she'd done up north?"

"Worse. She walked into one of the TV stations. Saleh, one can do that in Sadr City among our own— maybe! But Baghdad is a city that dies a thousand deaths every day. It is still a divided city. She was followed, I'm sure, once she came out of the station. They got to her by the Queen of the Rosary Church not far from here. I'm sorry, my brother. I have never failed so hard. I did not watch her carefully enough."

I was the one who had failed. Maybe in Tuz Khurma she would have had a chance. Maybe the documentary would have turned Zahra the Beheader into a genuine heroine. Some country or other would have even given her a visa . . .

"Here." In Jasim's hand I noticed several notebooks. They looked familiar. He handed them over. "They came for you."

Syria. Moalem's painstakingly tedious notes about defending a useless red house at Khan-T.

Jasim sang another classical verse: *"Such times when I struck my sword on the waves of mortality."*

"Do you know, Jasim, my left eye and right eye see the world as differently as the moon and the sun? I am mostly blind in the left eye."

"And that has something to do with what?"

"If I close the right eye and look at the river with the left eye only, all the garbage in this ancient river could be diamonds."

"But they are not diamonds. There is no romance to them. We Iraqis have to live here, you know. You are only passing through."

We were silent awhile.

"Tell me, how many ways are there to die in Mesopotamia?"

"Six thousand years passed, brother Saleh, and we are still counting the ways."

Afterward I went to the Queen of the Rosary Church alone and walked around. Somebody had left flowers in a corner of the sidewalk and I wanted to believe it was for Zahra the Beheader. Two men, guards, watched with curiosity and then with some alarm as they saw I was hanging around outside the church too long and not going away. There had been dozens of bombings in the area.

I walked off.

There is a window of time to grieve for others. And sometimes you have to shelve it for another day. Other times you have to do the grieving now and be done with it because there won't be another time. I'd had no ideas for Zahra other than to try to take her away from this country. But she had neither a passport nor the proper identification (the enemy had seen to that) to get her a passport anytime soon. It meant that this thin attempt at kindness had been a pipe dream. I had unwittingly left her in Baghdad to die. She had been a walking time bomb with just enough notoriety to get herself assassinated.

Back on Karada Street that night I drank copiously to her, to Zahra.

She had made a promise. If I managed to take her away from this land, she'd always, always bake us fresh bread. I would not grieve for her again, not like tonight. There were other martyrs on the way.

7

The domes shimmered on the canvases. I had never seen Miss Homa's meticulous brushwork so kinetic. She'd pushed past seventy many years ago and I would have thought time would have eventually caught up to her. Time instead seemed to have turned on her afterburners. Back in the day she had picked lovers like grapes. Yet she never married. Always stayed "Miss Homa," even during the darkest days of the revolution when she could barely afford her electric bill. Hers hadn't been a rescue from obscurity but a chance at a second coming. It had been, like so much else with art, a matter of timing. Timing and profit. Now the world wanted her. People bid absurdly for the painted domes that just a few years ago no one would look twice at. They came to her door. Invited her, to no avail, to hideously wasteful parties in a country where every five minutes, on the dot, I would watch another hungry face stick their head in the corner dump by my synagogue.

Those domes were divine things—mosque interiors of earth color and turquoise. Her ancient house, right off Sheikh Hadi Street, a fifteen-minute walk from my own place, was built around a shallow pool. They didn't make them like this anymore. This was old Tehran. Away from the soulless cubes of the nouveau riche north of the city.

She could afford to live anywhere now but she stayed put, faithful to the house that had been handed down to her by her ancestors.

She came into the living room carrying a tray of tea and pastries. It was raining and just before coming here I had finally finished reading through the war diaries of the martyr Moalem in Syria. Moalem's last sentence: *God willing, death will be as perfect as a glove.* I remembered the two of us in the red house. Moalem shelving his angry prostate and his wheezing chest for those minutes so he could defend nothing and no one, shouting for me to clock my rounds. How did one have a death as "perfect" as a glove?

Miss Homa had something to say about that. That was the reason I was here.

"You will take me with you over there next time. It is where I wish to die."

"But you may not die, Miss Homa. You may live yet for a long time. Imagine all the amazing art you'll produce."

She looked at me with a mixture of pity and annoyance. "Art?"

"Yes, it's what you do, after all."

She regarded her domes. In other rooms there were other canvases that spoke of other decades. Her lifelike, almost photographic portraits of personalities from the end of the last regime and the beginning of the revolution now brought considerable sums in the art houses of Europe. I had gotten a taste of all that right here in Tehran and across the Gulf, where young Arab princes showed off who could bid higher for her newest works, the domes. It was a world so far from where I'd just come from that even now I felt I was coming apart at the seams. I had sat in auctions in Dubai and Sharjah and watched money move like a virus. Everybody was dirty and my assignment was to be present and write about the "quality" of the works of art. A lot of the people in those rooms who bid on the art would be in other rooms the next day sending money for one side or the other fighting in Syria, in Iraq, in Libya, in Yemen. And so it endured, the imposture. I'd get invited to dinners at restaurants on Sheikh Zayed Road where they brought lobster and sushi not on trays but in crates the size of golf carts. I was a part of it. A small cog in the pageant of Middle Eastern excess and injustice.

They, the billionaires, had made a racket out of the twilight of Miss Homa's life. Yet the money she made for herself went to nursing homes, to orphanages, to hospitals, to teaching Afghan kids how to read and write, to war veterans, to families of martyrs. There was good in the world and she was it. Had I been a Tolstoy I would have put it down in a sprawling, all-encompassing book that took in the kitchen sink in this grand, fucked-up country and the countries around it. But I wasn't a Tolstoy, rather just another scribbler—as my mother called me—trying to make ends meet.

"Did you know," Miss Homa said, "I hired an accountant for exactly three weeks to help me give away all the money I've been making? I found out he was already stealing from me. Now I do all of it myself. It takes more of my time than the painting. I spend more time over ledgers and lawyers than anything. I told my studio assistants to go away and not come back. I don't paint anymore. I am finished."

I wasn't sure what she wanted me to say. I tried cautiously, "It's life, Miss Homa."

"An ugly life. But I've lived it a long time. I want to end it."

"End it?"

"And you are going to help me."

The latest grotesque shopping mall on Hafez Avenue was between Miss Homa's place and my own. There were several new restaurants on its sixth floor. After that last bout of mock interrogation with H, I'd gone there on my barbecued-liver binge. Now it was kebab that I wanted in copious quantities. The favor Miss Homa had asked of me was beyond the pale, and I had no idea what to do with it.

So I ate. Like Saeed and I ate in East Africa all those years ago. Around us there was unbearable hunger, but all we really cared to do at the Iranian Red Crescent headquarters was stuff ourselves and keep away the famine. Twenty years later in Iraq it was the reverse: it was the scale of the food waste that was a mind fuck. The mokeb casually threw away enormous amounts of food. The kind of absurd waste that only an army is capable of. Sometimes when a village was freed from the enemy and I stood in the back of the truck and distributed goods to the villagers, I imagined I was making up for all the discarded food in Arabia. But you cannot make up for that kind of waste. It was another kind of illness that went untreated because everything was ill. It wasn't just the Americans who wasted. We all did. We all were guilty.

"I was wondering how the food is here."

Mafiha spoke. My boss! Atia's "husband."

He was the last person I'd expected to see. The kebab lodged in my throat, I waited for him to speak.

"Atia told me you were back in the city."

"I guess now that she's your wife she reports to you. Chief!"

"Why do you not like me, Saleh?"

"I like you well enough, chief."

"Then come back to the *Citizen*. The art section awaits."

"You only want me there because Miss Homa talks to me and doesn't talk to you."

"Speaking of which, you just came from her place, didn't you?"

"I would say: 'Can't a man go anywhere in this town without being followed?' But the answer of course is no."

"What does she want from you?"

"It's our business."

His baby-bulldog face went green a bit. He had a full mane of graying hair he was proud of, always running a hand through it like one of those rock stars you see on foreign TV.

"Then don't call Atia again."

"Why not?"

"Because she's my wife and this is the Middle East."

"Oh. I thought this was Norway. I'm sorry."

"Don't be so foolish, Saleh. Atia begged me to come talk to you—"

I didn't let him finish. "Oh? Begged you to come talk to me? Here in this restaurant? And just after having me followed from Miss Homa's house?"

"We'll get to Miss Homa another time. For now I

want you to come back to the *Citizen*. It's a promise I made to Atia and I'm sticking to it."

I thought of Atia and my anger turned soft. Then the softness became unmanageable. I relented. "What if I said yes?"

"Great! You can start tomorrow."

"Can I eat in peace now?"

"Of course not. You've left a trail of angry people by disappearing like you did. As usual! I don't know why you do these things. But there are two gentlemen here to see you besides me." He pointed outside to the pizza house across the sixth-floor hall of the mall.

I was too blind to discern the faces of anyone from that distance. But I already suspected who they were. I had begun referring to them as Ajooj and Majooj. The TV writers for the *Abbas: Sniper Legend and Fist of God* television series.

"You owe us twelve episodes of *Abbas*. And starting next week. The public demands it!"

Ajooj and Majooj were types from central casting and they were inseparable.

Their ponytails were precisely the same length. Both were stocky in a squarish sort of way, but they comported themselves like art house film connoisseurs who had to write for TV in order to get by in expensive Tehran. They wore "natural" loose fabric clothes, always white, that made them look like vegetarian weightlifters, and they sent their kids to the same expensive after-school language programs. In other words, they had everything figured out, except that they didn't know how to bring the ratings up for the *Abbas* television show. I could not easily tell the two of them apart, unless they began to talk. "Italian" Ajooj had spent a few years studying in Milan and faked a preposterous Latin accent while speaking Persian.

I'd known these guys from our university days. They'd gone the way of anyone who has too little talent and studies film—they'd started a film festival business. But then bigger fish had taken that racket out of their hands and they'd signed on with Iranian television, where you could write about love triangles with zero sex from one season to the next and get paid for it. The *Abbas* serial was their big break. They'd ridden its crest this far and they didn't want to lose it so quickly.

I almost wished Mafiha had stuck around. Compared to these guys, at least he understood his own corruption; he took himself with a grain of salt. One time I'd asked him why all of a sudden he was writing antiwar poems and he'd said, with a perfectly straight face: "Because women like it and men can't argue with it." Now this very same guy, an editor in chief and art collector, Mafiha the purveyor of peace, was the guy who had my Atia. While I was left with hate e-mails and messages from pacifists who believed that even so much as reporting from Iraq and Syria was tantamount to murder and that I should be blacklisted from the peace-loving literary community.

I said to Ajooj and Majooj, "Did I sign anything that says I owe twelve episodes of *Abbas*?"

Italian Ajooj spoke: "No, but you will. Because State TV will be at your door and you know what that means."

"Well, it won't be so good for you guys either."

Majooj: "Just write us a few episodes. Give us some bullet points. It's all we ask."

"I'll have to go back to Iraq for research then."

Ajooj: "You're not going anywhere. You just came from there. You've had all the research you need."

"What if I don't write so well?"

Ajooj: "Then I'll personally bash your head in for creating a character you can't sustain. The whole country will hate you for it. We'll make you the most hated writer in Iran. The guy who turned the *Abbas* show to shit."

"I just wrote a pilot for it. I never meant for it to get so out of hand."

Majooj: "But now it has. And the O Channel demands that the show go on. You're responsible for it."

I stared at my hands. Once again, I could not get these thoughts out of my head: My brothers in Syria and Iraq had died so these guys could have their hit TV show. So Mafiha could be feted in Frankfurt and Amsterdam for writing "with a human voice." So Dodonge could publish a book about himself as "the true voice of Syria." And, finally, so that Saeed could chauffeur Europeans around for their weekend documentaries about combat.

I wanted out.

8

Nevertheless, within a few weeks the show's ratings were already up. Ajooj and Majooj turned out to be better writing partners than I thought. I would give them the most absurd ideas with just a few pointers and they would run with it. Suddenly the entire machinery of State TV and the O Channel were pulled into gear so that episodes could be filmed on the fly and shown as early as two weeks later. It was a record-breaking production time and Ajooj and Majooj were the faces behind the resurrection of the *Abbas* show.

Strangely, I had not heard from H, but he was certainly on my mind. So I took the show back to 2006, just as H wanted: The Americans are all over Iraq and Abbas the sniper legend, who is called into action from one of his many retirements, decides to give them a bloody nose for their perfidy in his beloved motherland. He begins taking out select individuals from long distances in Baghdad through his immaculate aim. Abbas can't miss.

The flashback to 2006 on television was a particular hit. Ajooj and Majooj became actual stars.

That was when I finally began to receive messages from H. It was obvious he had been reading the Marcel Proust book in his possession and he would send, via text message to my new phone, peculiar sentences that seemed like his own out-of-context ideas and mutations from French, via English, into Persian: *Gilberte is not unlike an unstable country with whom you should never form an alliance.*

One time I replied with a simple: ?

And he came back with: *D'Argencourt appeared gentle, since he lacked the physical ability to express that he was still rather mean.*

I wrote back: *Your English has improved so vastly that you are able to read this stuff and understand it.*

H: *But my writing in that language is still poor. Too poor! And my true wish is to be able to read it in the original French.*

Me: *Next lifetime, inshallah!*

H: *All of humankind is in this book, you know.*

Me: *Appears that way.*

H was taking credit, alongside Ajooj and Majooj, for the *Abbas* show's success. As my handler, he could explain to his superiors that it was really via his insistence that I come up with a new pilot for the war that the show had been given new life. Those Marcel Proust sentences he was sending me via text message were his way of expressing that he approved of the TV work, but he still hadn't forgotten that sooner or later I had to get back to Iraq and find the actual owner of the volume.

One day I found an old, translated copy of the novel in a bookshop near the University of Tehran. It was a fair translation of Marcel Proust into Persian, not great but not a disaster either. I bought it and went straight to a line I vaguely recalled.

I wrote to H in the Persian translation: *The nature of the moment meant that he had to entertain a mediocre crowd.*

To which H replied in English: *It felt fraudulent, like a book written in forced vernacular.*

When I wrote nothing back, he added: *A book with theories in it is an object that still displays its price tag.*

Of all the people in Tehran, my interrogator had become my one and only interlocutor, my savior. My saint.

Writing seemed to matter after all. It wasn't all lies. And even if it was, then you could examine that lie, work it, and stitch it into the fabric of your truth.

One day, as I was putting together the unlikely sixth new episode of the *Abbas* show about how the Iraqi sniper hero was visited by a man with angelic white wings who gave him a rifle with a special scope (made in the City of Brass at the far reaches of the Muslim Middle Ages), I received an e-mail.

Even now, as I write these words, I shudder to think that I might have been making the Iraqi champion into a cartoon figure, or a stock character from *The Thousand and One Nights*. My only consolation was that all the martyrs we knew were somehow turned into cartoons anyway. Go into any city where martyrdom is not an idea but something tangible, something that is of the mud and earth of that city, take a careful look at the faces of the departed on their memorial posters as your cab travels from the airport to your hotel room—in Tehran, in Baghdad, in Mashhad and Basra, martyrs posing with their weapons and other accoutrements of their death—and your mind will settle on how their absence has become a force of nature. The shadows of the departed hang over these cities not like saints but mood regulators.

The e-mail I received, like much else in my life, had to do with a piece of writing. It went back to a time when I'd been thrown into exile at the city desk at the

Citizen, that section of the paper which held far more readers than art but no personal profit.

The e-mail was in English: *I am a scholar interested in the old Jewish quarter of your city. Your article about Haim Synagogue across from your apartment piqued my interest. I would like to pay you for some research, as I am unable, due to political circumstances, to come to your excellent country.*

I shut the computer down, turned the lights out, and stood by the window in the dark. I'd never thought of Iran as "excellent," but that was one way of looking at it, I supposed, if you'd never been here. Was this a new trick by H? Had the man no other cases to handle but mine? He was breaking protocol by sending text messages. Now this e-mail.

I didn't want to think about these things anymore. Through the slats of the window shutter I watched the quiet garden of the synagogue. Everything was still and I had forgotten the seasons. It was neither hot nor cold, neither raining nor dry. It was nothing. A stillness was everywhere and there was a lull in everything. Did it even matter what season it was? Maybe even the war, which I hadn't the stomach to read about if I wasn't there myself, was over. In fact, it was as if the war simply never was and all along it had been a figment of my imagination. Meanwhile I was going through the routines of daily and weekly life in Tehran—visiting my mother, who was slowly losing her awareness of the world and barely registered my presence, spending a couple of hours a week with Ajooj and Majooj at State TV to come up with the latest illogical adventures of Abbas, and I had even begun the art column that Mafiha wanted at the *Citizen*. Whenever I entered the offices of the paper

I'd see Atia in the film department, looking fairly satisfied with her choice in life. I would see her in the hall-
ways when she and Mafiha happened to run into each
other, their quiet understanding and laughter: they were
in one another's orbit; they had a union and were on the
same team. I had put away my feelings for Atia a long
time ago, shelved them. Which was just as well. It was
Mafiha who had the woman, the position, the prestige,
and even the invitations abroad for his empty poetry.

Because I was quietly jealous, I threw myself into
work more than ever. The Middle East was in flames, Iran
was utterly broke, yet Tehran was bursting with art gal-
leries and art shows. Women and men were making their
fortunes overnight. There were exchanges of money that
boggled the mind even as our currency plummeted right
into the sewer. In such a world, why not make cartoons
of people? Maybe I would never even return to the war.

But I knew that sooner or later the war would return
to me.

And it did.

The impossibly tedious diary of the war in Syria that
I had inherited for editing from the martyr Moalem was
put into circulation just as fast as the *Abbas* episodes
were coming out on the O Channel. Overnight the diary
became a best seller in the provinces. I was sure the government was buying up all the copies to make the thing
a quick hit; it made for good propaganda. I did not care
one way or other; I would not even get a "thank you"
for my labors except the regular editor's fee, which was
a joke. But the publisher would score a fortune and so
would the martyr's family.

And what about the other martyrs of that fight in Syria?

Even in death some people were luckier than others.

At the *Citizen*, Mafiha seemed chirpier than ever. All the young women at the literary desk paid him more attention now that he was at last married and supposedly unavailable. He bantered with them and went to the gym and then to the sauna with the heads of the Censorship Department every afternoon to plead our cases. He was a hero, because everyone assumed that he fought for us to be less censored by the powers that be.

This all was a losing fight on my end. It was no fight, really. The fight was in northern Iraq and Syria and Yemen, yet I was here and didn't know why. Men were dead and when I remembered them I had a moment's pause, nothing more. My grief did not plumb deep enough to know tears, and even if there had been tears—in the way that people went on and on at martyr ceremonies—those tears would have been artificial, manufactured. I thought of that other martyr of the Syrian front, Nasif, who had pretended to be an Afghan: a man goes to the lengths of pretending he is from another country so he can go and fight a war and he gets killed for it. The mayor's office and the Martyrs Foundation were not even giving him the benefits of a proper martyrdom back home. They had decided not to put up posters for him since he had gone to Syria to fight as an Afghan under false pretense. They would have to put up his posters in Afghanistan instead, which was beside the point, because over there no one would remember him or cry for him. He had never even been to Afghanistan. If there was ever a catch-22, this was it: Nasif went unremembered in two countries because at the end of his days he had belonged to both and neither.

During this time I received another e-mail from the scholar who could not come to our "excellent" country. I still had not answered this entity, ostensibly a woman, and had no idea what to say to her. The safe thing was to say nothing and forget it. I had had enough trouble from H about writing a short story where my neighborhood synagogue made a cameo. To go researching for a foreign scholar about the old Jewish neighborhoods of Tehran while this war was still on and while I was a part of it, I just didn't know . . .

But what if she was genuine? Her reality played at the fringes of my mind. And each time I drove the thoughts off.

More weeks passed. The first showers of the season came to the north end of the city and one could glimpse snowcaps over the mountains surrounding Tehran.

It was Atia who finally broke the ice on the ground floor of the *Citizen* one day. She asked about my bad eye and wondered if I needed recommendations for a good doctor.

"I can see again, somewhat, if that's what you're asking. Turns out what I needed is this special eye drop. It's very expensive. You can only get it in the black market. But now that I'm working under you, I can afford it. So, thank you, I suppose." I started to go.

"Saleh, are you mad that I married or mad that I married Mafiha?"

I looked around. No one was supposedly watching and of course everyone was. "Is this a conversation we should be having now?"

"Probably not."

I motioned to leave again.

She said, "There's something I must tell you."

"Another bombshell?"

We stood there for a moment and I recalled something. We had been in the middle of a combat operation with Cleric J and the other men of the mokeb tagging along, when a bomb blew up right near me. Beautiful green smoke enveloped everything. Just then I was doing something that no one in their right mind should have been doing at that moment: I was on a cell phone talking to Atia in Tehran. It was suicide, but this was far from a professional war and everybody and their mother was on their phones anyway, taking self-portraits of their own goddamn demise. My ears were ringing and I spoke into the phone: "Atia, I think I just died. I'll call you later."

I was convinced there had to be a giant round hole in my stomach. I reached and touched myself. Everything was there, no missing body parts, no bleeding out, no shortness of breath or feeling cold. I should definitely not have called Atia again, but I did. "Atia, I'm not dead."

She had cried into the phone.

"Another bombshell, yes." She glanced away from me on the busiest floor of the *Citizen*, swallowed hard, and said, "Mafiha is coming out with a new book."

I shrugged. "Man's a regular factory of new works. When is he *not* coming out with a new book!"

"This time he has a coauthor."

"Nice. So you guys are already writing books with one another. I thought you and I would do something like that one day. But I guess the Book of Life had other plans for us, Atia."

"Don't philosophize."

"All right. So who's the lucky man or woman he's writing this book with."

"It has already been written."

There was a long pause and I waited for her to go on. But she just stood there. I remembered her when she was fresh out of the university. Young girl from the provinces. Full of ideals. Those first monographs she'd written for the Martyrs Foundation—they had changed the equation. It was the first time someone had written about our war heroes not as flawless, but as men who had greatness and not such greatness in them, warts and all. She'd received a lot of flak for it. The Ministry of Censorship wanted long chunks of the books out, but Atia stood her ground. She'd fought to explain that heroes would be that much more interesting if we saw them in their entirety and not just as removed icons we could not touch. They'd eventually listened to her, because Atia was that kind of woman. She did not back down. She was the one who asked the hard questions when she went to interview the "big men" of the regime. She had upended the landscape of biographical writing in this country, and she'd done it single-handedly.

What was she trying to tell me now?

"Atia, you can either tell me or not tell me who the lucky coauthor is. It really doesn't matter. It's not my concern."

"Dodonge."

"Him?" My voice cracked. "The charlatan of the Syrian front?"

"It's not what you think."

"It never is. But what *do* I think, my dear Atia?"

Just then Mafiha appeared by the exit. He looked our way, smiled, and went to the elevators without stopping. I felt nothing.

Atia said, "You think I sold out!"

"There's nothing to sell. Everything has already been bought and sold in this country. I know a lot about that. I'm an art reviewer, don't forget."

"You also write about war."

"Oh that! I guess I lost my way for a while. I would ask you what their book is about, these two brilliant gentlemen. Let me guess: one of them is prowar and the other supposedly against it. Wait! Is the book some sort of debate then? Like a meeting of two great minds debating a subject?"

"Yes."

"Ah, well. These guys really do know how to catch a tailwind."

"Saleh!"

"What?"

"There's something else."

"I'm listening."

"The *Citizen* is being bought out."

I'd already done six art reviews for them. This would be the seventh and last before the *Citizen* changed hands and we all left en masse. This sort of thing happened so often that Atia and I and the others were used to it. Some merchant or politician with ten thousand kilos of dirty money under his mattress would come in and buy out wherever we worked. Then he'd oversee everything we did because he wanted the paper as a platform for his political ambitions. Sooner or later, working at the journal or newspaper or publishing house would turn to shit and we'd all leave anyway. The only good thing that came out of this was that we were savvy now and did not linger until things turned nasty. We left immediately.

This was going to be my last review. The show was being held at Tehran's Modern Art Museum. I gave Mafiha the slip and went alone on opening day, even though I was almost certain Miss Homa wouldn't be there for him to try to hustle. Miss Homa never came to these things.

I was wrong. She was there, waiting.

"You have been avoiding me."

"Miss Homa, it's not every day someone asks you to kill them."

"Is this what I asked of you?"

That day I'd visited her, she'd said she wanted me to take her to Iraq. To Karbala, to be specific, so that she could die there. But she wasn't sick or dying, I'd reminded her. She'd smiled to that. Then I saw the halo, like the ones I saw hovering over every single martyr-to-be that I'd come across in my life. That certain shimmer that tells you the person is ready to go. At first I put it to the blindness of that left eye. That world of exquisite dancing lights which sometimes softened the blows of life. Even when Atia had told me that the *Citizen* was being bought out and that Mafiha and Dodonge were coming out with a book on war and peace together, I'd observed how much better it was at times to be half blind that way. Not fully, but just enough to see the world through a prism that took away its ugliness a little. As if one were looking at it all through one of those kaleidoscope tubes we used to twist and turn when we were kids.

"Why Karbala?" I hadn't asked the question that day but I asked it now.

And her answer was ready-made: "Because of Imam Husayn, the grand martyr."

"Miss Homa, you've lived one of the fullest lives I know of. Now you are suddenly religious?"

"It has nothing to do with that. And it has everything to do with it."

During our chat people kept coming up to her to congratulate her on the show. It was a group event titled, *Women of Art over Five Decades.* But because this was her moment, even though there were eleven other artists in the show, a good half of the spiral space of the museum had been dedicated to her work alone.

"Why me? You could snap a finger right now and half of Tehran would jump at your command. They'd fly you to Karbala first class."

She looked tired and thoughtful. She began to say something, but just then I saw Mafiha appear from around the corner. People stood in groups, chatting, pretending that even though death was everywhere they were still not alone, that they were with friends and that this was an important event. Instead of plastic cups of wine they held grape juice in their hands, they smiled vacantly and nodded their heads, they pointed to this or that canvas and said things.

I didn't know what they said. I had done something I'd never forget or forgive myself for. When they brought Ali-Akbar's body parts out of that school, I had been filming and talking into my camera. Had I known that leg was Ali-Akbar's I wouldn't have erased the video.

But I'd erased the only final memory I had of the martyr. Him with his baggy military shirt because he hardly ever ate. Just skin and bones really. Skin and bones and the best damn shot in a company of snipers. Dead because he stepped like a fool over a trip wire.

Mafiha pulled up alongside us and beamed at Miss Homa.

"This is my boss," I said with practiced respect in my voice. He was Atia's husband, after all, even if he wasn't technically my boss after the sale of the *Citizen* was complete.

Miss Homa nodded.

Mafiha switched gears into his usual chatter and I lost the words. Something about wanting to do a complete sketch on her for an art magazine overseas, France maybe, or the United States. My mind drifted. I thought of the British writer Graham Greene in the Suez reporting during a war. Getting shot at grew tedious after a while. He became bored. War was mostly boring. But it also depended on a lot of other things. You can't get bored when somebody is screaming *Allahu akbar* from two hundred meters away and vowing to cut off your head. Boredom has no place there. Boredom runs away, because you can't.

When I moved back into the conversation, Miss Homa was talking.

"Which part of my negative answer do you not understand, sir?"

"I know people abroad, Miss Homa," Mafiha said. "The article I'd do would—"

"Would what? Make me famous?"

"Miss Homa, you already are famous."

122 ⌣ Salar Abdoh

"Increase my prices?"

"Well!"

"Not interested."

Mafiha was smart enough to know when he was rejected. He bowed and removed himself. More people came over. More deference toward Miss Homa. It was like watching an opera.

I said, "All right. I agree. I'll take you to Karbala."

"What changed your mind all of a sudden?"

"This place. It's horrible."

"Saleh, I will explain in more detail why I must go. Please come see me this week. When do you think we can leave?"

"When the ratings of the *Abbas* show on television reach the moon."

"Is this a joke that I should understand, Saleh?"

I watched her. I thought I knew why she wanted to go to Karbala. In the winter of her life she had suddenly become too famous. What was she going to do with this fame so late in the game? It was almost a slap in the face.

I said, "It is only half a joke, Miss Homa. I'll visit you next week. I promise."

"I want to be over there for Arbaeen."

I had been hoping she wouldn't say that. The thought of Miss Homa walking alongside ten million other pilgrims converging by foot on Karbala on the fortieth day of Imam Husayn's martyrdom didn't suit me at all.

She seemed to read my mind. "If you don't take me, I'll go by myself. I'll get a plane ticket to Najaf and walk the seventy-five kilometers to Karbala with the pilgrims."

I stared at her some more, believing every word she said. "That does not give us much time."

"Less than three weeks."

"You seem to have everything worked out."

"At my age, one does. There may not be a tomorrow."

"You still have not told me why you wish to do this."

"Do you ask this of every pilgrim?"

"No. Only one pilgrim. You, Miss Homa."

"When you visit me next week, I will explain. I will have our tickets ordered for Najaf by then."

I started to object, but then saw there was no point. A light peck on the cheek and I left her to the admirers who were waiting to move in for small talk and signatures.

There was nothing I liked about this museum. It was a prerevolution structure that they said was a copy of the famous Guggenheim building in New York. I thought the place redundant and the stuffy spiral architecture more like a giant human aquarium. Still, the place carried one of the richest contemporary art collections ever assembled anywhere on earth in its basement; it came from a time when the country had been flush with new oil money before the revolution.

My phone rang. It was Cleric J from Iraq. Not a good time to answer a call from the war.

I got a glimpse of a burly artist I'd written poorly about two reviews ago. He made three-meter-long eyesores of nothing but black paint, and just the word love inscribed in a corner of the canvas in the thuluth script of Arabic with gold letters. The review had brought in a string of phone calls to the Citizen and physical threats. They were mostly from collectors who saw a bad review as a drop in their investment.

I decided to make myself scarce.

Outside, Atia and a group of theater actors were chatting away. I tried to shove off, but she'd seen me.

"You've barely been here."

"I'll come back when it's less crowded."

In her hand she held a postcard-sized invitation. It was for the Mafiha-Dodonge "War & Peace Talk" in a bookstore the next evening.

I pointed to the cards. "You are really working hard for your man, aren't you?"

"Wouldn't you?"

"What are they going to talk about? That there are two sides to a story? That sometimes you need to have war, but that peace is really much better? Could have fooled me!"

"Why do you always have to be such a killjoy?"

"You know, your husband just tried to work Miss Homa . . ."

"And?"

"She'd have none of it."

Atia laughed. "He tries too hard sometimes."

"Just sometimes?"

"I'll put your sarcasm down to your hanging around so many dead men. It can't be good for your mind, you know. You are an encyclopedia of trauma."

"I don't have any trauma, Atia. My only trauma is that you went and got married."

She pointed to her theater friends. "See all those people over there? They all say you're working for the state promoting war. They say you're an informant. A stooge. A warmonger. An opportunist."

I knew most of the people she referred to by face. A predictable lot. They never got tired of shoving Chekhov or Samuel Beckett down people's throats. Throw them in a real Beckett landscape, like the town of Baiji in Iraq after the enemy had finally retreated from there, and they wouldn't last half an hour. There's nothing more absolute than square miles of rubble after a prolonged battle. Nothing more soul-crushing and thorough. Beckett knew something about that. These people hadn't a clue.

Suddenly I wished Mafiha had given me the theater desk too. I'd know what to do.

"I'm an informant?" I shrugged. "Yes, I inform on war."

"You know that's not what they mean."

"If I'm an informant, what's Dodonge, your husband's new best friend? The guy has made himself a virtual hero on other people's miseries in Syria."

"Dodonge is different than people like us."

"Meaning he has never read Kant or Rousseau? Never worked for any literary journals?"

"Yes, something like that, Saleh." She shoved one of the invitation cards into my hand. "Come tomorrow night if you like. Or don't come. I don't care."

She walked away. Walking like a trailing oud solo behind the looking glass and beyond my reach forever.

Oh Atia!

I was being followed again.

I texted H: *The art of life is to reach the divine through those who make us suffer.*

He replied almost immediately, as if he'd been waiting: *To glimpse something anew is to revisit all that one's eyes saw the first time.*

H, I decided, had lost his mind. He was sitting in his interrogation room reading a mountain of a European book from early in the twentieth century. I wondered if he'd ever had to torture anyone.

Me: *Are you having me followed? Because I am being followed right now.*

H: *It's not us. It's someone from your own family.*

Me: *I don't have a family.*

H: *Certainly you do. Your mother is family.*

Me: *Well yes. But that doesn't really count. Besides, she is indisposed.*

H: *I am not talking about her.*

Me: *Who then?*

He did not answer.

I spent the rest of the night in the darkness of the apartment mostly staring out the window. The courtyard of the synagogue was like an old friend. Inside it the place was blinking. From its upper story the dimmed light of the chandeliers gave one a feeling of martyrs and magic and afterlife.

I went back to that first e-mail that had come from abroad: *I am a scholar interested in the old Jewish quarter of your city. Your article . . .*

I finally replied to the e-mail: *What can I do for you?*

Around three a.m. there was another text from H: *Don't e-mail this person again.*

I wrote: *Entrapment?*

H: *Not quite.*

Me: *Why are you helping me?*

H: *Because I don't like my life.*

When I opened my eyes at three p.m. there had been

fifteen missed calls on the phone. All of them came from my mother's nursing home.

"Is she dead?"

"Sir?"

"You people have been calling me nonstop. Is my mother dead?" I gave my name.

"There is a visitor. We cannot give out telephone numbers. So we dialed your number for them."

Since the Persian language lacks feminine or masculine pronouns, I had to ask, "Is *them* a man or a woman?"

"Man."

In an hour I was at the nursing home. My mother was staring vacantly at her Turkish soap opera. The woman next door who had relived the Bolshevik invasion every day for the last forty years had finally died. In her place they'd wheeled in an ancient Hungarian who kept asking, in perfect Persian, about tomorrow's weather.

On the other side of bed sat an owl of a man. His eyes were fixed, hardly batting an eyelash. Avesta—short, fifty, neurotic, and always looking slightly desperate despite the fame he'd manufactured for himself abroad—stood up and came at me with a handshake that felt like a knife. We did not like each other and were make-believe cousins by obligation because of my mother's second marriage into wasted wealth. Even his name gave me hiccups, one of those pre-Islamic decorations that the rich always like to give their sons and daughters. Whereas I'd grown up in near poverty, Avesta and his kin had gone to the best schools abroad. Francophones to the hilt, they went out of their way to show they did not mind you being French-illiterate. But of course they did mind. A lot. And I had always been that poor pretend cousin whom they kept at a distance, but not too far because, after all, I did write for the papers for a living. They might need me sometime.

Avesta needed me now. That attempt at a handshake gave it away. He would have air-kissed me otherwise.

I reached over and kissed my mother. Her reaction was slow but definite. "Why have you no hand?" she said. Then her head swiveled just as slowly and she zeroed back in on the television. She was a blank. I was losing her the way you lose a toy you stopped playing with years ago.

"What can I do for you?" I said to the pretend cousin.

"You have to write an article and take everything back about what you said regarding that Homa woman."

"Miss Homa to you."

"Whatever. She's becoming too famous outside of this dump of a country and—"

"It doesn't suit you?"

"Because of what you wrote, everyone here thinks I stole my dome and minaret paintings from her."

"Well, the domes you did steal from her. And the minarets you stole out of inspiration from the domes. So technically you are a thief."

"A curse on you, Saleh!"

"But no worries, cousin. In art everyone is a thief. I don't see why you've come all the way from—wherever it is you live now, Paris? Berlin? New York?—come all the way here to this, as you correctly put it, dump of a country to complain about an article no one cares about."

He stared at his invented aunt, my mother, as if he needed a witness.

There are people who want and want. I had spent

the last years of childhood being invited once in a blue moon to this family's immaculate homes in the north of Tehran where they kept pristine swimming pools even in the worst days of the revolution and during the war with Iraq; I'd been relegated to the kitchen to eat with the servants while my mother worked to ingratiate herself with our new rich relatives.

This world was empty that way, and a man like Avesta still wanted to have more of everything.

Avesta gestured at me to follow him outside. He didn't say anything until we were well beyond the walls of the nursing home. Across the street two men sat in front of an expensive-looking Citroën. One of those men was Saeed, my backstabbing filmmaker partner. He didn't get out of the car.

I said to Avesta, "It was you who was having me followed yesterday. You could have just knocked, you know."

"What about that article you are going to write taking back everything you said about Miss Homa's work?"

I started to repeat my usual line, that I was just a poor writer and that my words were not even worth the paper they were printed on. But he stopped me.

"I'll pay you. I'll give you two paintings."

Avesta had been trying forever to make a name for himself beyond, to him, the lowly Middle East. But when middle age came and he was still not considered a tier-one international artist, he'd settled on the art markets of the Gulf where he too was followed by Emirati collectors the way Miss Homa was. With our currency's value plummeting as it was, one of his paintings could now buy me an apartment here. Two of them could buy me two apartments. I could rent out both of them and not have to think about writing art reviews anymore.

I had to get him off my back. "All right. I'll write something."

"When?"

"What's your hurry? Miss Homa's not feeling well anyway. The poor woman will probably die soon."

"No!" he shouted. "She can't die. Not now. If she dies, her prices will go through the roof and . . ."

I was no longer listening. I was thinking of Miss Homa. Our vocations of martyrdom had prices and estimates, it seemed. The war too had turned into an auction. And the martyrs were the works being sold.

9

Cleric J stuck close to the ground in his faded blue tunic. He could have been a nineteenth-century dervish in an Orientalist painting selling spiritual mumbo jumbo on the pilgrimage roads of Western Asia. In his hand was the AK he seldom used but kept close. Maysam, a mountain of a man and Cleric J's head of security from Amara, lay twenty meters to our right. Maysam had the face of a bear and when he smiled it was ample, as if the world had opened up at last and it was a holiday. He was frowning now, telling me to keep my head down. He swore something in dialect that I didn't understand.

Cleric J laughed and said in his singsong Persian, "Saleh, you are trying too hard to become a martyr."

The whiz of bullets split the air, sometimes so close they were whispers an inch away. This had been going on for an hour and I was bored at last. And uncomfortable. The ground was mud; detritus from weeks and months of stasis was rolled into the landscape, making it resemble some kind of death-paste. The Kurds stayed at Bartella and bided their time. There was an unspoken border between us and it wasn't really unspoken. In the middle sat Mosul, waiting.

Cleric J was in his element when he was getting shot

at. Tranquility graced his face. He looked at you with clinical eyes, as if to say: *Watch, because if this is my last moment, I want you to know and tell everyone I gave it my all. I will go with a smile on my face.* I envied him that. I'd left Miss Homa down south in Najaf and told her I'd be back in a few days. A week had gone by, and the enemy's reinforcements were suddenly like genies out of thin air. It made us wonder if the Americans were not playing us. Maybe they had an entire army of these men under lock and key and were dispensing them in paces just to test our will and kill us in easy-to-deny numbers. Whatever it was, it worked. Men got tired and jumpy. This corner of the war should have been over. I'd come back after three months and not only had we not budged, but now they were raining rockets on our positions. The Kurds, God bless their grit and spirit, occupied the heights and were not unhappy to see us softened a little. There would be reckoning later.

The beauty of all this, and also its silliness, was that the distances were a tease and I could still check my e-mail through the Iran data plan on my brand-new phone. And so I did. A mortar round fell to the right and Maysam cursed again. In fact it wasn't a curse at all but something with God in it. It wasn't quite prayer either.

The talk from other dugouts reached us in spurts:

"Why can't they call a gunship? It's a lone position."

"Because they're all busy with Tal Afar."

"My brother is getting married after Muharram."

"I can't afford to get married. They haven't paid us in two months."

"I'm not coming to the war anymore if they do us this way."

"It's that thief, Abu—they say he has friends in high places in Baghdad."

Someone moaned. Shrapnel.

"Professor, do you have pain pills?"

I looked into my pack and saw cold medicine. I tossed it over. "Take two."

"Who just said he is not coming back to fight? We're not here for money . . ."

"*Li beyk ya Husayn!*"

"*Li beyk ya Husayn, li beyk ya Husayn!*" we all shouted back.

Sometime later two rattling armored vehicles went right up to the enemy nest and blew it to pieces. The whole thing was so anticlimactic and unheroic that I didn't bother to go over for a look while everyone went on shouting *Li beyk ya Husayn*. But as I continued to scroll through useless e-mails on the cell, a text message came from H.

H: *O Channel says you haven't sent anything in the past week for the Abbas show.*

Me: *A little busy at the moment.*

Maysam was shouting for everyone to come over to where the nest had been. We all got up and walked dutifully that way. We were tired of the enemy. Tired of their clever bunkers and their tenacity. Most of our Hashd forces could have been home this evening for dinner. Instead they were here in this camel's ass of a no-man's-land trying to smoke out remnants of a dwindling war. Maysam pointed to a hole in the ground where the enemy had scuttled back and forth over the past few weeks. Cleric J was on the phone, hearing it again from a commander—exactly what was the reason that the people of the mokeb had to be out here engaging the enemy? Cleric J gave his usual beautiful and dubious lecture about the burden of those who were living, and that we'd really come so far out because we'd heard there were villages that needed feeding. It was untrue, of course—no villages here. Cleric J had been itching for a fight and the men at the mokeb were depressed from the previous two days and nights of rain. Nothing like getting shot at to remind you of the blood running through your veins. Cleric J was a therapist at heart.

H: *Are you still there?*

Me: *Please transmit the following to O Channel: Abbas falls in love.*

H: *How?*

Me: *He meets his match in a woman sniper near Hawija. He stalks her for days and finally has her in his sights as she is drawing water from a spring. He does not pull the trigger. She is . . .*

H: *Beautiful?*

Me: *Majestic. O Channel will have to find a suitable woman for the part.*

H: *They won't go for it.*

Me: *The writers, Ajooj and Majooj, will have to deal with the Censorship Department. That's not my concern.*

H: *Ajooj and Majooj?*

Me: *The cowriters. It's my name for them. You'll know who they are.*

We lost connection for a minute. I looked around. In the time I'd been typing messages back and forth to H, a man had gotten blown to pieces. There was a lone tree and he'd gone there to take a piss and stepped in the wrong place. I closed my heart to that and did not go near to take a peek. There had been an explosion and

I'd certainly heard it. But you get inured to it. Hard men were shouting hard words in Arabic. That broken tree was going to have pieces of the dead man hanging and dripping from it for a long, long time. It would be near impossible to get it all off. I already knew all this and forced myself to not be curious.

H: *Any news from the enemy scholar?*

I was confused for a moment and wrote, *Enemy scholar?*

H: *You know, the OTHER enemy. Not those prehistoric fools in Iraq and Syria.*

Me: *YOU told me not to write to her.*

There was silence. And silence from H meant this: *Don't you ever use capital letters like that with me, boy!*

I wrote meekly, knowing full well that he already had the information and was just testing me: *The answer is yes. This other enemy—she asks that since I will not answer her, perhaps I can recommend someone else who will do the research she needs in Tehran.*

H: *Tell the scholar to meet you in Erbil.*

Me: *What?*

H: *Do it. Erbil is a taxi ride away from you!*

Me: *What, take a cab through enemy lines?*

H: *Don't play stupid. You know what to do. Do it!*

Haji Yusuf came up to me looking glum. "I keep telling the young men not to just walk around as if this is their father's backyard. To God we return!"

"To God we return, ya Haji Yusuf!"

And then we both turned and saw our world. Maysam and the bomb-disposal guy in the middle of no-man's-land. The disposal man digs his hand with its two missing fingers into the ground and slowly picks around a diameter. This is nothing like the movies. Rather, it's

as if he's a child—and he *is* a child, twenty at most—
looking for treasures of the Median armies who passed
this way before time. Soon he has a barrel next to his
feet and is explicating on it quietly to Maysam. He walks
not nearly carefully enough some paces, digs again, and
comes up with another barrel. Then another. And another. It's a mine highway. It's a painting. It's midfield in
a football stadium. It's many things and giant Maysam
and the bomb-disposal boy stand there and look toward
the horizon, while Cleric J talks into the phone telling
other commanders other things they should know about
the location. From all of these barrels they'll extract in-
cendiary material and reuse it for rockets. This war may
be stupid but it possesses genius. Meanwhile, Cleric J's
faded and muddy blue tunic flaps magnificently in the
wind. The awkwardly built armored vehicles, looking
like mud-caked lozenges, rattle their way back down
the road to their own shitholes, oblivious to the miseries
they have set in motion.

I wrote: *Do you continue not to like your life?*

H did not answer.

That night the big guns aiming toward Syria would not
give it a break. Unable to sleep, I walked across the
road to where Khaled used to keep house and where
Ali-Akbar and the Three Magi of the sniper team would
come every afternoon unless they were pulling duty at
the sater. It seemed like a lifetime ago. In real terms
only a few months had passed. Nostalgia can blanket
a man when the people who populated the dangers he
knew are no longer there. I knocked on the door and no
one answered. But people were staying here. Recently

washed clothes hung from clotheslines. I knocked again and when there was still no answer I let myself in. Same room. Nothing had changed, except for the fighters who lived here while the war continued. In a corner the same mattress lay where Shorty, one of the Three Magi, had taken a long sleep after his best friend Ali-Akbar's martyrdom. Shorty was a compact twentysomething from Qom whose prayers tended to go on interminably. That day, the way he slept after Ali-Akbar was killed, it was as if he were cleansing himself of something. When he woke up it was like he'd slept a thousand years and during that time he'd made many ablutions. We didn't talk about Ali-Akbar again until Tehran.

I crawled onto the mattress and closed my eyes. Before long there were men in the room. All of them young Iraqis. Their AKs hanging off the same hooks where Khaled and Martyr Ali-Akbar and the Three Magi used to hang their weapons. The television was on. This was new. There hadn't been a TV before. And they seemed to clearly receive the channels broadcasting from the Gulf. I sat in silence alongside the other men watching a Hollywood movie in English with Arabic subtitles. Every single actor in the film looked astounding, the women and the men. A story about a future world where survivors of some catastrophe live in a bubble and the heroine is mermaid-like and more beautiful than anything in *The Arabian Nights*.

We were mesmerized. Just a few kilometers from the sater we sat watching the world of the beautiful. Their fictions broadcasting right into this broken room that the enemy almost managed to capture some months ago on their way to steal fuel they needed to get them to the capital of their fictitious empire down the road in Syria. I do not know how to translate any of this. I do not know in how many worlds a person can live simultaneously before they lose themselves completely. There is not language enough to explain all of this.

So I sat and watched the film to the end. And when it was over somebody turned on the lights, food was brought, and everyone came over and kissed the new guest twice on the right cheek as if I were their long-lost brother. No one asked who I was. They'd only seen me across the road at the mokeb serving tea and rice and chicken to their brothers, and that was all they needed to know.

I wrote to H: *Tell O Channel that they must end the Abbas show with his falling for the enemy sniper woman. Abbas and the woman begin a cat-and-mouse chase that is their version of a flirtation. The flirtation of the best two snipers in Iraq. But in the end, one of them has to kill the other. This is the law of this land. And it is not the man who kills the woman. It cannot be.*

Men dispersed for sleep now and I saw that light was seeping from underneath the room already thick with the breath and snores of those who'd been on first night watch. I went outside. Across the road the mokeb had come to life. Haji Yusuf, Maysam, Cleric J—everybody was out front serving tea and dates and calling out, *Shabab, shabab, hala-bikum, hala-bikum.* The machinery of combat was unwrapping itself for the day. The morning freeze of northern Iraq chilled the bones and men jumped off personnel carriers with cold faces, rubbing their hands together to take their bitter tea with mountains of sugar. There was nowhere else I wanted to be on this earth. The big guns aiming for Syria still hadn't quit. They were annoying, like dogs when they go on too long.

I went back to Khaled's and into the kitchen where it was still too early for anyone to barge in except for two men who went back and forth catching up to their short morning prayers. I wrote quietly for the next hour, drawing out the contours of the *Abbas* tragedy for the TV show's finale back in Tehran. I was filled with doubt again. The writing life in my corner of the world, except for brief interludes of good, had turned out to be not just a disappointment but a tectonic lie. This realization was so all-encompassing that little could be salvaged from the rubble.

Even Iraq had turned into a lie—here, where men would take their tea at Cleric J's mokeb in the morning and be dead by nightfall. I had, disgracefully, turned Abbas, the great hero of Iraq, and his life into shit, like everything else that was turned to shit here. I finished the bullet points and segments of dialogue for Ajooj and Majooj and the O Channel and sent it off to H this time to transfer to them. Someone had begun blasting martyr songs from the fuel depot. The songs and the rhythmic chest-beating of tens of hundreds of men was hypnotic. A remarkable symmetry and adoration. We all were itching to be back down south, in Samara, in Karbala and Najaf, taking that long walk of the martyrs for the Arbaeen pilgrimage ceremonies. It was surely more habit than belief, because our ceremonies of self-flagellation were really a mother song. We'd been born into it and this time of year was to have been ours. Instead we were here, fighting an enemy who wanted to make short work of us. At the same time our vigilance made us believe our sacrifice was on a mythic scale. We thought that we were not just fighting for ourselves but for eight billion souls. Because this enemy meant to destroy the world with its talk of jihad and its persistent suicide missions in all the major capitals. If anything, the Americans and Europeans should have feted us, lionized us, given us compensation and weapons for our sacrifice. What we got instead was their aversion. Because we did not look like them. Because we could afford to die in large numbers and they couldn't. We convinced ourselves of all of this even if it was only half true and sometimes not true at all. Yet we wanted to be understood and appreciated. We were ruined and romantic at the same time. There was a reason that Lawrence of Arabia had gotten carried away with himself in these landscapes and wrote about it as if he were writing about something divine. He had come into contact with that touch of the divine about the Arabs—no matter which side of the fighting they were on. Their dignity was like skin; it never wore off, even when they had to turn to infidelity. In all of these ways they were different than us Iranians and the fighters from other places. They honored The Word and what it could do. They were born into poems and they died there; poets all, from day one.

By the time I got back to the mokeb, Maysam was beside himself. He came up and gave me a good shake. "You are alive!"

"Shouldn't I be?"

"Saleh, don't ever leave the mokeb again like this. Don't go without telling us." The concern in the big man's face was of a scale different than I'd ever seen.

"I always go away and come back. What's different now?"

"The enemy."

I waited for him to explain.

"They've put a prize on Iranian heads."

This wasn't news. It had been the same in Syria. But I'd always thought of it as the unlikely thing that happens to the next guy. It was too much like the movies and I didn't want to buy into the fear. But I could see his disquiet wasn't going away. I said, "It's different here, Maysam. The good Iraqi people won't sell an Iranian out."

"Don't be so sure. When the prize is high and—" he pointed to the bleakness that was everywhere, "when this hell is what a man has to wake up to every day, he will sell his own brother. Trust no one outside the mokeb."

I nodded. Maysam was our mother and father here. Sometimes he got so pissed off at Cleric J's recklessness that he dared to do what no one else did and screamed at the fighting cleric. Those were the best of times and we all sat back, grinned, and bet on who'd win that round.

"I hear and obey." I turned to go toward the big pots to start the rice, but he held my hand.

"There is something else."

Death, in all its colors, immediately hovered. We had all become connoisseurs of this sentence—*there is something else.*

"Someone has been martyred?"

"Your three friends. The *Irani.*"

I looked at him nonplussed.

"Martyr Ali-Akbar's friends from before," he added

by way of an explanation that I didn't need. He was speaking of the Three Magi.

"But they were not supposed to be here," I said weakly. "They were back in Iran."

"Arrived two days ago. Friendly fire." He pointed skyward. "Air. Seven more from our own Hashd men were also martyred with them. They were inside . . ." He pointed to a large concrete drainage pipe sitting on the side of the road. "Inside something like that, I believe."

This added detail, for some reason, was sickening. Not the friendly fire, which happened all the time, but that they'd been inside some big tube. Why? I was boxed into this little detail and couldn't get out of it. Nor could I understand why the Three Magi hadn't made contact with me when they'd arrived two days earlier.

"Do you want to escort them back home?" Maysam asked.

"Is there anything left of them?"

He nodded. "Enough."

The rest of the day I sat on the roof of the mokeb's long-house watching convoy traffic outside and mokeb traffic inside. There was a lot of agitation. Three white-turbaned, AK-carrying younger clerics from one of the farther out-posts came up and consulted with Cleric J. Their sater had been penetrated yesterday. The enemy had a thing for saddling their pickups with explosives and looking for weak spots in the line. Once they thought they'd found one, they came at it with a single-mindedness that made the toughest men holding the line pray for their mothers. It took only one guy getting over that hump and blowing himself up inside the trench to birth a dozen martyrs, if not more. The hump was everything; once you were over it there was not a thing anyone could do. The already-dead bastard was not there to use his weapon. His weapon was to blow himself up, which was next to impossible to stop.

Blame seemed to be going around today. Everyone drank their tea and said God's name too many times. The Americans were always the object of derision in these conversations, their occasional air support for us questionable at best. On the surface we were fighting on the same side for a change, and against an enemy that wanted the earth itself to be gone. Over at places like Palmyra in Syria and Mosul down the road from us, the enemy had gone on orgies of destruction of all things ancient, afterward gloating in their sick cruelty over priceless historical stones that could not fight or talk back. No wonder then that in the mokeb, and up and down all the saters of the war, we quietly saw ourselves as the soldiers of civilization, even if no one else believed us or gave a shit. It was not something that was talked about. But it was there. In the air of every minor battle. And in the newscasts out of Iraq too. This was Nineveh, after all. The ancient capital of the Assyrians. The Nineveh of the Bible and the vast 2,700-year-old stone tablet library it had once held. We were certain we were fighting for something bigger than just Mesopotamia. And we were eating the bullets that the Americans, who despised our skin and our faces and our weapons, should have been eating right alongside us. The Americans saw us as rodents, and we saw them as a hollow Goliath. They laughed at our poetry and "queer" dancing in the middle of war, while we wept and held wakes after their friendly fires that killed our brothers. I wondered if anything, anything at all, could ever bridge these suspicions. I wondered if the so-called friendly fire that had killed the Three Magi had not only been the Americans but also thoroughly calculated.

Still, even if we were to find out the truth about the murder of our boys, what then? What could we do with that information?

Not much. I'd gradually come to think of them—the Americans—as entities beyond the realm of touch, or comprehension. Now and then we would run into their convoys on the trunk roads of Iraq. We passed one another like ghosts in the afternoon. Their equipment and vehicles had the feel of high walls with no human beings visible from our vantage. They were extraterrestrials to us. Here but not quite here. And sometimes I asked myself if we too were not just as invisible to them.

I stared at my buzzing cell and put it on speakerphone. Atia was quietly crying.

"Dear, I don't have enough money on my account here. If you're going to cry, please hang up, cry to your heart's content, and call me again later."

She stopped. "You are a fool, Saleh. Do you mean you are over *there* again?" When I stayed silent she said, "I take that as a yes. Who are you in competition with? My husband?"

"Atia, please forgive me, but . . . fuck your husband!"

"That is my job. Not yours."

"That hurts!"

"Good! I need to talk to you."

"Well, I'm here and you're there and my phone will go dead in a minute if you don't go and put money in my phone's monthly balance. I can't do that from here."

I waited for her to call back. Haji Yusuf waved at me from the tea stand he had set up across the street. Men huddled here and there over small fires warming their hands. The guy I called Egyptian Mo was teaching several young Hashd warriors how to do a headstand. He lined them up against the bullet-riddled metal of an old rattletrap and patiently went through the motions of showing the proper placement of the hands and the initial kick to get themselves upright. It was almost pastoral, this image. Except that about fifty meters away an old man walked in their direction with two sheep. My initial reaction was, *What if he's carrying? What if in the next half minute Haji Yusuf and Egyptian Mo and the Hashd boys become scattered body parts?* The old man and his sheep approached and passed, quietly and without fuss. Just a straggler who had been left behind when the last of the villages in the outlying areas were liberated.

There was clapping of hands from the Hashd boys as Egyptian Mo stayed in position on his hands, then twisted around, did a flip, and went up again repeating everything on just one hand this time. It was a performance worthy of a champ. I thought: *I have no idea what has brought Egyptian Mo all the way here from Egypt; I have no clue what has driven him to become one of us instead of one of them. Is it his love for the story of Imam Husayn's martyrdom? Is it a love for the underdog?*

I knew nothing.

Why did we fight? I had believed I knew. But I didn't. Why did any of us come back to this godforsaken spot over and over again? Why did old Haji Yusuf personally put that North African enemy combatant out of his misery back in early autumn? Haji Yusuf could have just as easily let someone younger and more enthusiastic do the killing. Why dip your hands in blood like that when you don't have to?

Minutes passed and still no Atia. Maybe she'd never call again. Maybe she'd fall into the sinkhole of a Middle Eastern marriage like many a good woman.

I had a flashback of her while I remained there on the mokeb roof—a last glimpse of my beloved on the night of the Mafiha/Dodonge book launch back in Tehran. The two men holding forth like they were UN emissaries. It was a reunion of a lot of people I knew from work at the *Citizen* and also from other papers I'd moonlighted at during the past few years. Book launches in Tehran were at best an inglorious failure. But not this one. Book City on Shariati Avenue had a line snaking outside. Did people care so much about books on war? Or was it Mafiha's peace hokum they'd come for? Interrogator H was there too, reckless in his desire to be anything other than what he'd been hired to be, a feared agent of the state. If he continued like this he was bound to get fired, or worse; you didn't just walk away from a job like that, and you certainly didn't show your face so freely at public events like this, since there were bound to be people there whom you had interrogated at some point. I'd always thought that what H really desired was reincarnation; now I was sure of it. He was a burnt-out case, his job a burden. I saw him perusing the young adult section and moved quickly away, only to catch sight of more folks from the *Citizen* between the Western art and philosophy bookshelves. A little farther down was an entourage of war veterans, some deliberately still wearing combat fatigues. No doubt Dodonge had brought them along for show, as a part of his ongoing bravery extravaganza. The vets shuffled uncomfortably next to psychology and social science, looking out of place but enduring. They knew everything that was happening here was because of them; they were the spark for it. They were doers, though now diminished, serving as background decor for a piece of theater that had nothing to do with the war and everything to do with two men's literary ambitions.

When the program started, with Mafiha reading a poem that began with *"Peace has a price,"* I shut his bullshit out and focused a little more on the faces of those veterans. I was sure they were men who'd known combat maybe as recently as last week. But without their weapons they were ordinary civilians who did not know what to do with their hands. They were childlike and their vanity had been crushed. Yet their faces betrayed a knowingness devoid of the zest that ran like blood in the civilian audience's impenetrable wall of smiles. It was then that I saw Shorty, one of the snipers of Three Magi fame who would soon be dead, alongside his comrades.

Shorty's nose was in a book that looked to have been borrowed from the photography section.

"What are you doing here?" I asked him.

He didn't seem surprised. "Saleh! We're on our way to *jebhe.*"

When a man says to you that he's headed for the front, you enter another region with him. It is as if everything you say to him or hear from him no longer quite belongs to the realm of life. I could not have known that soon Shorty would be dead from friendly fire inside some industrial barrel on the Syria-Iraq border. And like most of those deaths, his death too would have little to no color for me, because I would not be close enough to witness it. It was like being cheated out of real lamentation. One minute you are making rice at the mokeb and the next minute somebody comes up to you with the familiar words: *Something has happened.*

"Your boys are with you?" I asked Shorty.

He put the book away, a collection of war photographs from the 1980s. "No. I came alone. They advertised this thing tonight in Nights of Damascus."

Nights of Damascus was an online group that all the Defenders of the Holy Places veterans subscribed to on their cell phones. Mostly pictures of martyrs on the Syrian front, but not Iraq. It made me guess that Shorty and the others were soon headed much farther west than Tal Afar.

"Well?"

"Well what, brother Saleh?"

"This event. What do you think of it?"

He looked genuinely perplexed by the question. "Nothing. That Dodonge guy, he is a fake. The other guy, I don't know him. He doesn't look right either."

We stood there for another minute listening to Dodonge pontificate on the sacrifice of our boys in Homs and Damascus and Hama, rattling off place names he could be sure everyone understood. His eyes welled up with tears. Those tears would sell a lot of books tonight. Then Mafiha came back with another poem. This time he was likening peace to a mother waiting for her soldier-child to return home. The mother is by the river drawing water while the sound of guns echo from the other end of one of the two great rivers of Mesopotamia.

"*Kos o she'r*," Shorty said.

"Yes. He is a shit-talker for sure."

We instinctively made our way toward the exit, pushing past former colleagues I had to nod to and smile at.

Outside, Shorty lit a cigarette and said something under his breath. I could not make it out. He looked totally glum. He said, "You know, the government is not giving Ali-Akbar his martyrdom benefits."

"It's not like he exactly needs it now," I joked tastelessly.

Shorty spat. "You know what I mean, Saleh. His family. His mother. The man even had a wife."

"Are you going out to defend the holy places for the sake of the fringe benefits, or are you going for Imam Husayn?"

"Come on, Saleh! A man needs to feel some support in his death! Some martyrs get their faces on posters every year and their families get allowances for life. Others, like poor Ali-Akbar, may God have mercy on him, they don't even get two words of thanks from *you know who*. You should write something about these things in the paper."

"Is this why you showed up here tonight?"

He didn't answer.

"They'll hang me by the balls, Shorty, if I write about stuff like that."

He spat again. "Then what's it all for? What are we doing all this for?"

"I don't know. You tell me. You guys are the ones

going out there without the right permissions from the Guards. You guys head out there alone and then get yourselves killed. But it's the Guards who have to practically glue you together and ship you back home so your mothers can mourn over you. You ever think about that? Maybe that's their way of saying, *Whoever goes to fight without permission can look forward to an afterlife of obscurity and zero martyr benefits.*"

"That's not fair."

"Not much is."

Shorty's eyes twinkled. "But we're going legit this time. The Guards came calling after we came back from Tal Afar. They're the ones shipping us out. They need guys who can carry the load, if you know what I mean. And they know we can. We proved it to them in Iraq."

"They're sending you to Syria, though, aren't they?"

Shorty nodded. "Our war's almost over in Iraq. We need to graze elsewhere. You coming with us?"

"No."

"But you were there recently. What's it like in Syria?"

"Different."

"How different?"

"You have to watch your back in Syria. If the Syrians on your side tell you they'll cover your flank, it probably means they won't. There's brother against brother over there. It's different than Iraq."

"So what's a guy to do?"

"Cover your own damn flank."

Shorty laughed. "That's a good one. Best advice I ever got."

"Shorty . . ."

"What?"

"Your brother comrade, Ali-Akbar, there was no reason for him to step on a wire. You guys are better than that. Cover your flank, son. I beg you!"

"Saleh, remember that village? I came out of the schoolhouse for just one minute and *boom!* I'd stepped out for a smoke. I thought we were done in that accursed village. Now I have to live with this for the rest of my life. Ali-Akbar was my brother. With Imam Husayn as my witness."

"Don't worry. The rest of your life won't be much longer. Syria will see to that."

His face lit up, a mixture of worry and enthusiasm. He looked like a boy about to smoke his first cigarette. "You really think so?"

"Yes. So please take care of all your business that you have to take care of first. If you need to bequeath this and that to someone, do so now."

"A guy like me, what does he have to bequeath? You make me laugh, Saleh. I'm not educated like you. I finished seventh grade, that's all."

Later I'd find out that, officially, they'd put down Shorty and his two comrades as having been martyred in Iraq, not Syria. It had been a border operation. None of this mattered then and none of it would matter afterward. But at least Shorty's family would get the martyr allowance that Ali-Akbar's family would never get. Shorty's op had been official; Ali-Akbar's hadn't. It was another stupid toss of the dice.

"Saleh, let's find a mosque and pray together. For old time's sake. Two *rakats* each for the happiness of the soul of our brother, Ali-Akbar."

I pointed the way to the nearest mosque. "Do two

rakats for me too. I have a little business inside. God protect you, brother." I turned to go.

"Saleh!" I waited for him to speak. "One day at the Eye of the Horse we saw you bury a book. It was the first time you were there. We didn't know you then."

"So it was you guys who reported it!"

"We didn't know what it was. We dug it up. Just a book. But we didn't know what was in it. There was, you know, some other handwriting. But the book was English, I think. We didn't understand it. Ali-Akbar . . . he said it was our job to report it. Just to be sure, you understand."

"I understand."

"So what was in the book?"

"Wisdom."

"What did it say?"

"The man writing those words, he'd lived through a war too."

"Who doesn't?"

"He wrote that there's something cruel about the leaves they grant to the men at the front."

"What does that mean?"

"It means you should be in Syria right now. Or Iraq. Here, you don't belong. You need to be in the fight."

"From your mouth to God's ears, Saleh."

"Inshallah!"

Back inside Book City I hovered near the exit. I thought I deserved at least five minutes alone with Atia before I took off again for Iraq, not knowing what exactly I wanted to accomplish in those five minutes. I finally spotted her far from the stage they'd set for Mafiha and

Dodonge. People were clapping. There seemed to be some sort of intermission. Atia was busy ordering something at the café next to the magazine section. I didn't have the energy to trek all the way through that crowd. Maybe I'd join Shorty for those two rakats of prayer after all.

Then, as I turned to leave, I saw him. The same Beatles haircut. That astounded boy's face behind round, wire-rimmed glasses. You couldn't miss Daliri of Marcel Proust fame if you tried. I went over, grabbed him by the arm, and pushed him toward the door.

He was terrified. Turning around to object, there was an immediate hint of recognition in his face seeing me and so he said nothing.

I forced him to sit on the back of my motorbike and we rode into the night.

I knew exactly where I was going. I was going to Miss Homa's.

"Saleh, it's official. The *Citizen* has been sold."

Atia's voice was back on the line and it echoed on the roof of the mokeb longhouse. For a moment I was discombobulated, unsure where I was. I'd been so deep in my daydreams of recent events in Tehran that I'd completely forgotten I was waiting at the Eye of the Horse for Atia to call back from across the border. A text message had also arrived reporting that my phone had been recharged over in Tehran. It still astonished me that you could get an actual text message from another country while in a combat zone, informing you that your monthly balance was good and that you could even get a week's worth of free Internet if you punched in a few numbers.

I said, "Well, we already knew that."

"But it still hurts. So many of us put in a lot of effort into that place."

I had no sympathy—not for her or for myself or anyone associated with the periodical. True, it had been, hands down, the best paper around. But we knew that as writers and editors our lives were bound by a piece of thread. We had nothing that was ours. Even our writing wasn't ours. It was either commissioned, which made us drudges and hacks; or, even if the idea was ours, it still had to go through the obstacle course of the censor's bureau. We were liars. But mostly we just lied to ourselves, thinking that we were engaged in the life of the world, that we mattered, that we were somehow softening the ugly edges of living where we lived. But the good old censor always had the last word. That was a reality we would never escape.

Atia remained silent and so did I. Below the mokeb roof I heard someone calling my name.

"Do you have to go?" Atia asked.

I asked her to wait and peered down. A circle of people—Cleric J and several young men and another man I'd never seen before. The new guy with them was a bit disheveled and I could tell he wasn't one of us. Maybe he was around forty, maybe a little older. His eyes gave him away. There was irony in them and an acknowledgment of the absurd. *This man has to be a Westerner*, I thought.

I put out five fingers asking for five minutes. Cleric J nodded and the men walked toward the room I shared with the cleric in the back of the mokeb.

"Atia, did you only call to tell me the *Citizen* has been sold? Good riddance, really."

"How can you talk like that?"

"Easy. Everything is for sale. Even you, my very best friend. So why not the *Citizen*?"

"Have you considered that I might be happy?"

What if she *was*?

I was worried that this war would end and I'd have to reinvent the wheel of everyday life again. Some people, like Cleric J and Egyptian Mo, were already seriously talking about the next fight. Cleric J's words verbatim: *If we don't find martyrdom in Iraq or Syria, inshallah, there's Yemen.*

I thought about Yemen and Atia's happiness as a continuum, one long black-and-white reel beginning with devastation and ending in a marriage of convenience.

"I apologize. I am happy for you, Atia."

"Mafiha wants to quickly put a new magazine together and he'd like you to run the art section again, immediately. He's got all kinds of money backing him."

I didn't lose anything by agreeing.

"Fine. Tell him I'll do it. I'm not going to Yemen anyway."

"Yemen?"

"Nothing. Talking to myself. Tell him I'm on board."

"But there's a problem."

"I'm listening."

"There are two problems, actually. One is that your old friend Saeed has been making trouble for you. He's been going around saying all the story ideas you've sent for the *Abbas* show you stole from him. He's put in official complaints with several unions. And he also has that painter, your cousin Avesta—"

"That impostor is not my cousin."

"Whatever. He's got Avesta also trying to get you

blacklisted from working in media here. You are in deep trouble, Saleh, especially with the Journalist's Union. Unless, of course, you write another piece admitting that not only did Avesta not steal the ideas for his paintings from Miss Homa, but that in fact Miss Homa stole them from him!"

"So all of my troubles are about theft? Either I stole something or I falsely accused someone of stealing?"

Atia sighed into the phone. "You could say that. Yes."

"You know, our country is truly a work of art. Maybe I'll go to Yemen after all."

"Don't go down that road, Saleh. Please!"

"Fine. What's the second thing you wanted to tell me? Or was this all of the good news for today?"

"The second thing is that our mutual friend called me in for a talk." She meant H. "He also wants to know if I'm happy in my marriage. I told him yes. He seemed disappointed. Then he asked where the hell you were. You'd disappeared again, he said, and he hasn't heard from you for a while."

"He knows perfectly well where I am. He just wanted to see if you knew. But if it makes him happy, tell him I'm back where Marcel Proust was buried."

"Why do you talk in code, Saleh?"

"This is not code. Next time you see him, tell him I'm here where Marcel Proust was buried and that I truly miss our literary chats. He'll understand."

"So you'll work with the new magazine?"

"I already said yes. And, Atia, I'm truly happy for you and your marriage."

"What about Saeed and Avesta? What are you going to do about their lawsuits?"

"I'll handle them."

I had no idea how to handle them. But Cleric J's man was on the roof now, calling more forcefully this time. Apparently there was to be an ad hoc *ijtima*.

As soon as I'd bid Atia goodbye the phone's screen lit up again. It was a text from Daliri, my Proust. The message came from a new Iraqi number I'd given him: *Dear Saleh, Miss Homa and I are on the move. Please come to us before it's too late.*

10

I'd gunned the motorbike straight for Miss Homa's house that night after the war-and-peace charade at the Tehran bookstore. When Proust, riding at my back, tried to ask questions, I told him to shut up; I was the one asking questions. It was a role reversal of sorts—as if he was me and I was Interrogator H.

Miss Homa placed sweet mint tea in front of us and sat gazing at Proust. It was a curious look. She obviously could not decide whether she should be amused or angry at me for bringing a perfect stranger to her house at night. Proust, meanwhile, looked on in awe around the living room. Miss Homa's canvases, especially those domes and minarets, appeared to overwhelm him. In the days ahead I would come to know as much as there was to know about Proust. Born in one of the shore towns of the Caspian Sea, he'd scored high enough on his national exams to be accepted to the state medical school. But he'd opted for literature, the fool. After four years of reading the Persian classics and another four toward two higher degrees in French literature and translation, respectively, he'd finally landed back on earth to face reality—there was not a bloody thing for him to do to make a living. His family had supported him far longer than they should have and then one day told him to get a life. Which meant get married, settle down in small-town Iran, and, at best, become a bank clerk or a schoolteacher. I'd encountered dozens similar to this poor bookish fuck. I'd worked with them, heard them out when they contemplated suicide, and I had drunk to their afterlives once they'd hanged themselves or went missing or threw themselves under a truck. These were not the martyr types. They did not go to war. They read modernist European literature instead, in barely passable translation, and dreamed of other places—of Paris in the 1920s maybe, Vienna during the late Hapsburg period, or Madrid and Hemingway and bullfighting. They were budding Middle Eastern poets with nowhere to go, no visas to the West they could procure, no doors of the greater good world open to them. They had no money and they dreamed of ordering whiskey in a bar somewhere where there was a hint of freedom. They could just about taste that real whiskey that they'd never before tasted while simultaneously imagining writing the next great Persian novel, not realizing that the previous great Persian novel had never been written. And when that avalanche of reality one day finally came bearing down on them, they either got enough prescriptions of antianxiety pills to put a horse into a deep coma or else they jumped off a cliff. Usually they did both, though with a several-year interval of utter misery in between. That was Daliri/Proust in a nutshell. I'd had students like him at the University of Art in downtown Tehran. There must be a factory somewhere where they made the likes of him—with that bowl-shaped haircut and writerly glasses and hangdog look.

I did not want to waste time. "What were you thinking showing up in Tehran like this? You're supposed to be dead, son."

"No one knows I am here."

He had a way of withdrawing when he spoke, as if afraid he might get hit or run over. He was in his early thirties. I imagined during his military service he'd been the butt of everyone's jokes. They wouldn't have bullied him exactly, but they certainly would have made him pay for loving books and not being manly enough. He'd probably spent a lifetime being scared but chance had finally brought him a job working for State TV. He was indistinct enough that even State TV, which vetted your great-great-grandmother before refusing you a job, had taken him on. He was the invisible man incarnate. But one thing had led to another and now he was considered a martyr. His family would continue to draw a pension from his loss. He was at last good for something to them. All that French and Persian literature he'd studied! It took faking his own death to be appreciated in his motherland.

"Do you realize how much trouble you're in?"

"I swear, *Agha* Saleh!"

"No need to call me sir. Just call me Saleh. How do you know me anyway?"

"I used to read some of your dispatches."

I was about to drill into him again while, as they say, the oven was hot. But Miss Homa who'd been quiet so far, stopped me.

"Can't you see he is scared, Saleh? What do you want from him?"

I watched Proust and felt a pang of guilt. Maybe I'd been around men like Interrogator H and Cleric J and the Defenders of the Holy Places for too long. Hard men. I wasn't being fair to Proust. I stood up and asked Miss Homa if I could help myself to her bar where there was an array of liquor. When I came back to them they were quietly talking, as if they'd known each other forever. I'd been hoping for this, but to see it happen so quickly was still odd.

"Well?" I said.

Miss Homa looked at me. "Mr. Daliri here tells me—"

"Just call him Proust," I blurted impatiently.

"Proust?"

I nodded.

There was a look of shock in Proust's face, but he said nothing for now.

Miss Homa said, "Fine. Proust tells me that on the way to my house you told him he must leave Iran and never come back. Is this true?"

"Miss Homa, if they find this guy here, they'll—"

"I know, I know. He told me all about his recent martyrdom."

"They'll provide him with new identity, some money, even a job, and all he has to do is go back to Iraq and start a new life."

Proust shrugged hopefully. "It's not like I had a great life here. I hated my job. We made propaganda documentaries for stupid television."

There was a pause during which all three of us imagined the alternate lives we could have lived. Something was happening. A transformation and a coming into being of light at the end of the tunnel. But this light was the light of extinction, of annihilation. This was about dying. Call it martyrdom or whatever name you want to put on it. The colors in my left eye began to jump. Shafts of light going every which way. I hadn't been taking care of the eye again and now everything was a rainbow on a roller coaster. I saw Miss Homa, and to a lesser degree Proust, as bundles of moving light, as if they were saints in those Persian and Mughal Indian miniatures of old. Miss Homa glowed the way the soldiers I'd known at the front began to glow when the spirit of martyrdom came calling. At first I used to put it to excessive imagination. But later, when I talked to others, especially men who had fought in the eight-year war three decades earlier, I realized this was something you really did begin to see. You began noticing the signs of martyrdom-to-come. Its colors and variations. Its velocity.

Maybe getting left behind enemy lines was the best thing that had ever happened to Proust. Luck had made him survive the ordeal. The lines were still so fluid just a year earlier that you could walk half a kilometer and be on the wrong side of the war. Proust had walked, by utter chance, to the right side. The Iraqi Hashd men had taken him in once they found out he was Iranian. Somewhere along the line he'd left that book of his which I'd found and buried at the Eye of the Horse—the same book that Interrogator H was now steeped in. This toss of incongruity had no end and no one would believe it unless you were there and saw how allegiance was not necessarily to any belief but to the blood of friendship. I'd sat in that house across from the mokeb many times, when Khaled, a Shia Muslim to the marrow of his bone, somehow received word from his hidden-away Christian neighbors in Mosul about enemy troop movement inside the city.

"What about Marcel Proust?" I now asked. "And I don't mean you, son! I mean the real one, the writer. Mr. Marcel Proust, the Frenchman."

Proust stared back at me with that by now familiar look of frightened disbelief. He was a small cornered animal at that moment. I watched the halo slowly lift and disappear from him. I had perfect vision on him suddenly. It told me he was not going to be a martyr. At least not anytime soon. I was not sure whether to be happy for him or disappointed. I only knew I had to get him back to Iraq before the wrong people discovered him here. Miss Homa in the meantime sat back and watched our exchange.

I repeated my question. "What about Marcel Proust?"

"My favorite writer," he said hesitantly.

"Does one take this kind of writer to war?"

"I was not technically in war. I was with a film crew. But how do you even know all this?"

"Where do you think you are living, brother? The sixteenth arrondissement of Paris in the late nineteenth century? Don't worry about how I know all this."

"It is not a crime to take a book with you to war."

"It's not normal to take *that* book."

"Why not?" He seemed positively affronted now.

"Well, for one thing, it's too big. And elegant. And beautiful. And literary. It's a bloody masterpiece, isn't it?"

"For all those reasons I took it."

"And underlined a lot of it."

"That I did."

"Why?"

"Sorry, but is this some kind of interrogation?"

"Yes. Maybe."

"I underlined the book because I was trying to compare the outdated English translation I had on me with the original French that I'd already read."

"A regular scholar!" I scoffed.

"I've never read him," Miss Homa suddenly cut in. "Mr. Marcel Proust, I mean."

We both looked at her, surprised for an instant that she was even there.

I asked, "Why did you leave the book at the Eye of the Horse then? What kind of a man leaves a book like that in such a place? Are you mad?"

"There was an attack. We had to leave fast."

"I figured. But where did you go after that?"

"Karbala."

"Why Karbala?"

"Because . . . because I wanted to cry at Imam Husayn's shrine. I'd been spared certain death and I wanted to join him."

"You wanted to join Imam Husayn?"

"Yes, Imam Husayn. The greatest martyr of all time."

"You are lying. A man who reads these kinds of books doesn't go crying to Imam Husayn."

"Anything is possible, sir."

He was right. Anything is possible. Somewhere in the warped line of time, Imam Husayn and a European masterwork had come together. That was all there was to it.

I asked, "Did you go to Karbala instead of heading home because you knew they'd already made you a hero back in Iran? A martyr?"

"There was that too. I could not go back, could I?"

"So why are you here now? Why did you come back to Tehran?"

"No one knows I'm here. I've been staying in a flophouse in the Gomrok District. I got homesick. And I was running out of money. I saw a flyer for that event tonight so I went to Book City. I . . ." He hesitated. "I came back to Tehran because I don't know how to become a martyr in Iraq."

"Do you need help toward that purpose?"

He was silent for a while.

"Yes. I need help toward that purpose."

"So do I," Miss Homa murmured. "Please, gentlemen, drink the tea before it gets cold."

The three of us drank in silence. The person who desires obliteration will get it. Some are quick about it, some take longer than others, some hesitate, and some even lie about it because they are embarrassed to admit they don't want to die. It was often the talk of the trenches—exactly when a man should become a martyr. A volunteer to defend the holy places had a duty to do just that: defend. But you couldn't exactly defend if you were dead. So how did you negotiate the two and come to a concord between life and death? These are ultimate questions that don't get asked in peace, because peace means having to worry about the pair of new shoes you need to buy, or your kid's braces, or the milk going sour. Trench talk in Mesopotamia was different than other wars because the bluster of martyrdom was actually real. Even those men who didn't want to die had to talk the talk. And because they were there, sometimes, despite all their precautions, they became martyrs. They reached sainthood through a lie despite their every effort not to be saints. My concern was not these men, but the ones who walked into the butcher house willingly, knowing that there was a fifty-fifty chance there would be a video of their cut-off head posted online by the enemy the day after tomorrow because the op they'd volunteered for was outright suicide.

I tried to speak but Miss Homa hushed me. She had, she insisted, all the money she needed in the world. Her fame had reached its limit. And she was tired of this world. Her collectors had designs on her store of unsold paintings. After which she could die for all they cared, and in fact it was preferable from the collectors' point of view that she did. But she refused to do her dying on their terms; she would manage it on her own. Everything that was hers she'd already bequeathed to a number of charities. A lot of the unspoken-for works, her house, everything. There would be plenty of stealing by the lawyers that she'd put in charge, because there was always stealing. But her last act would be a *bilakh*, a finger, to the world. She was going to get her way into or near Karbala with or without my help.

Proust looked positively ecstatic hearing Miss Homa's words. The two of them were on the same page; they wanted to experience the rapture of being extinguished like two moths in a candle. They wanted to die together. It was their pact. It was serendipity. And poetry.

It was also madness.

"You both wish this because it is in fashion now. It's not something you can take back, you know."

"Don't insult my intelligence, Saleh. Will you help me?"

"To die in Karbala?"

Miss Homa nodded.

Proust turned to her, beaming. "I am your servant, Miss Homa."

"Think hard, young man. I can leave you something. Enough for you to live a sufficient life."

"No, I want what you want. I've already tasted it. Even if what I tasted was not real. I want to make my martyrdom real now. I cannot go back to what I had."

"But you can go forward."

"What would Imam Husayn do?"

"He would think both of you are mad," I cut in.

They looked at me as if bothered by my presence. I seemed to no longer speak their language. One of them wanted to die so she could smother her own late fame and be finished with it, and the other wanted to die because of a glitch in the apparatus of martyrdom that had made him a hero before he was ready.

I added, "Besides, neither of you would be considered martyrs that way."

"Saleh," Miss Homa said, "please stop talking out of your ass. Martyrdom is just a word I use. You can call it anything. Call it 'aluminum' if you wish. It doesn't matter to me. It is the act that matters."

"And I'm already a martyr," Proust said brightly. "I don't need to do anything but finish the job and earn my title."

There was nothing more to say. Neither of them could take an AK and defend a sater, waiting until a Toyota filled to the brim with explosives came crashing in. Yet they wanted what all the martyrs of Syria and all the dead Hashd boys of the land between the two rivers wanted. They just had to do it a bit differently.

"I need another strong drink," I said with resignation.

"Don't worry, Saleh," Miss Homa said, "I am leaving you something too."

I stared at her, waiting for her to continue.

"My biggest canvas that I still own."

"Your rendition of the Goharshad Mosque cupolas?"

"It's worth a good amount of change."

Proust was beaming again. I considered ringing his neck right then and not waiting till Karbala. He said, "Just think, Saleh, you'll be like Charon the boatman in Hades, and Karbala will be your River Styx."

"And we your passengers," Miss Homa pitched in.

Both of them seemed thrilled with this sudden Western classical allusion that showed off their learning.

"What if I don't do it?" I asked.

"You will," Miss Homa said. "It's your job. It's why you're there. It's what you do. You are our Charon!"

11

Cleric J said, "Saleh, I know you want to go down south for the Arbaeen pilgrimage. But we have to first find out who this man is. This man, Claude. He carries a French passport."

Cleric J passed the passport over to me. The fellow was certainly photogenic. A little older than I'd imagined when I first glimpsed him from the rooftop of the longhouse as they accompanied him across the mokeb. Forty-six, to be exact. An angular face. A voluminous shock of hair with stylish hints of gray. He looked distinguished, unhappy, highly intelligent, and enigmatic. What he was doing in northern Iraq by the Syrian border, and on the completely wrong side of things, none of us knew. Cleric J seemed to think I could find out. I understood what the issue was. This man, Claude—Claude Richard—could have been with the Kurds who would have welcomed him with open arms, like they did with all the Westerners who came to join them in the fight against our common enemy. There he would have found those poster-perfect Kurdish female fighters too. He would have enjoyed no-strings-attached American air support and adventures of a lifetime to write home about. Why had he come here then? Our equipment was mostly hand-me-down, our blankets were infested with

fleas; out here hardly anyone spoke anything other than
Arabic and occasional Persian, and we were mostly just
lurching our way awkwardly toward our own escha-
tology. We were waiting for the Messiah, the hidden
Twelfth Imam of our faith. We were busy flagellating
ourselves and crying over Imam Husayn's death 1,400
years after the fact. We didn't want intruders. We didn't
want anyone to come study us. Fuck you! We wanted to
be left alone to deal with our enemy, and yes, we'd take
a little air support from the Americans now and then
rather than have them kill us. Other than that, go away!
That's why there were no foreign journalists here. We
would not have said no to them coming around. But we
preferred they didn't, and that's what they did—they
didn't come. Because it was uncomfortable here. And
dirty. And not cosmopolitan in any way. We were war's
guttersnipes and dog soldiers, despised by the corre-
spondents who filed their reports from comfortable oa-
ses like Beirut and Istanbul. We didn't mind. What we
minded, what I minded, was this Claude Richard. His
first and last names were two first names. What was that
about? It seemed made-up. Yet the passport was real and
so was the fact that he was here at the Eye of the Horse.

"Where is he now?"

"They took him to have a meal."

"God is great!" I offered.

"God is great!" Cleric J chimed back.

Now Maysam came into the room, towering above
us. He peered down at me and Cleric J and ran an index finger against his own neck, as in cutting someone's
throat. It was a question—one that at the same time was
both innocent and brutal.

Cleric J said quickly: "*La, la*. Not yet!"

Both men turned to me.

I swallowed hard, turning to Cleric J. "You are going to put me to the test again, aren't you?"

Maysam answered, "You can talk to him in his language, or some language, and tell us if he is a spy."

"He doesn't look like one. And even if he was, look at us! What is there to spy about here? We have been just sitting around for weeks and weeks eating onions. We haven't moved."

Cleric J began adjusting his prosthetic leg. "Listen, this is what we do: we find things out. One day this man just shows up down the road in Tal Abta and says he wants to sign up. Are we a circus that he showed up like this? Do I look like a donkey, Saleh?"

"God forbid! You are a great man, sayedina."

"Then go talk to him. Find out how he got as far as Tal Abta. What he wants. And why he is not somewhere safe and warm."

"And if he answers wrong?"

Cleric J undid his prosthetic leg and waved it in my face. "This is a war, not his mother's lullaby. Now hurry. *Yallah!*"

H's text message said: *Why have you not answered my messages?*

Me: *You told me to go find the Proust guy and I went to find him.*

H: *He is at the Eye of the Horse?*

Me: *No, I've left him down south.*

H: *Why?*

Me: *He loves Imam Husayn.*

H: *Don't be a fool, Saleh. What do you mean?*

Me: *I mean exactly that. I've left him in the south because he's in love with Imam Husayn. Aren't we all?*

For a few minutes a steady hail of bullets came into the defunct fuel station on the halfway road to Wardiya and then stopped. The place was a lone, long-abandoned empty depot in the middle of nowhere. It was walled in, but still in the open and vulnerable. A chubby man was bleeding from the thigh and I watched Claude bandage him up for the ride back. Maysam was shouting at someone walking toward the kiosk where normally the stationmaster would have been. The man stopped and turned around, looking befuddled as if the dangers of booby traps were just tall tales from other places. He was one of those people from Kut who did not say much and had damaged skin. He kept to himself, read the book of the sayings of Imam Ali, and wept. His weeping was infectious. It made other men weep too, and I wondered often what anyone in their right mind would think if they saw our mokeb on the move. We truly must have resembled a circus, despite Cleric J's protests to the contrary. Maysam continued shouting at the poor man. Our head of security's gruffness while on the job was only matched by his tenderness when he was back home with his family. He became a teddy bear then, spoiled his little daughters, wore his caftans and held court like some benevolent minor king on holiday. Cleric J was no different. The kids from his second wife could have been his grandchildren, but at home he was out there every afternoon playing ball on his one working leg while men stood twenty-four-hour guard outside since infiltrators in Diyala had sworn to assassinate him. It was a special kind of madness, all of this. It turned grown men into adolescents and for a lot of them the fatwa from the grand cleric to stand up against the enemy was really just that perfect excuse to get out of the dreariness of domestic life.

Cleric J shouted into the walkie-talkie: "If we try to take off now we'll be left with a martyr or two."

Most of the men appeared like life-size question marks just then, lowering their centers of gravity, convinced that a bullet would somehow miss them if they walked around as if they suffered kyphosis. The bullets had felt random and I didn't have eyes nearly good enough to notch the distance. It was the luck of the draw and if you heard a bullet go past, it was already gone and you had nothing to worry about. If it caught you, you still had nothing to worry about; you were done. This question of luck always lurked in the back of the mind. Two years earlier when the war was still in its infancy and the enemy was winning, we'd gone with Saeed up to nearby Lalish to film the Yazidis. They were a curious people, their religion reaching so far back into the bowels of Mesopotamia that they seemed hallowed simply by surviving as long as they had in this unfriendly land. I could not get a handle on their faith but they were unbearably handsome and utterly decimated, the enemy having reserved a special kind of savagery for them. By a little rock formation at their holiest site in Lalish, an old holy man handed me a common towel and said this was their wishing well. If one threw the towel at the rocks and it did not fall to the ground, the wish would come true. The only wish anyone had at the time was to not be slaughtered a few kilometers down the road. How was one to reconcile the fact that the enemy was closing in, the Yazidi men had been butchered by the thousands and their women and children raped and sold into slavery, while here we stood trying to throw a goddamn face towel at a holy rock formation? The Middle East was dying. It was dying right here too in this forlorn outpost in the Nineveh Province, where we imagined bullets would not catch us if we made ourselves small.

Claude said, "Have I passed the test now?"

"What test?"

We were back at the mokeb. Cleric J had gotten an earful from the commander who was charged with flushing out the enemy on the escape routes past Wardiya. I did not know how to negotiate this man, how to write about him. There was no interiority to Cleric J. He carried his tasks of looking after the fighters as if he were possessed, pumped with supernatural drugs. The commanders gave him a talking-to each time and it made no difference. They needed him, so they didn't berate him too much. When there was an especially dangerous mission, he was one of a handful of guys in Nineveh at the time who could rouse the fighters, bring them to a fever pitch. He could have said Imam Husayn was riding a white horse on the horizon, and yes, men would have braved the rockets to follow that imaginary white horse toward perdition. How could you scold a wild, lovable holy man like that?

Claude smiled. I didn't know where it had started, but someone had called him the Father of the French, *Abu Faranci*, and the name had stuck. Abu Faranci had quickly become one of us. He spoke English with a deep, almost antiquated inflection and volunteered for everything. He was up before everyone cleaning the mokeb and at nights he cooked long into the evening and then washed the pots and pans. The men couldn't communicate with him but they offered him genuine smiles. They came right up to his face and sang him the breathtakingly heroic and improvised Arab poetry of war and he grinned back and said, *Allah, Allah!* He was in his element here, like Cleric J. Our merry gang had needed an Abu Faranci to be complete and it got one.

Abu Faranci said, "Cleric J took us out there today to see if I didn't mind getting killed. It was a test. Yes?"

"Everything is a test here. You could say yes. Yes."

"So what else would you like to know?"

"I believe you have a few brain cells missing, like the rest of us in this mokeb. But I don't believe your story that you just showed your journalist's ID and managed to get as far as Tal Abta. Not on your own, anyway."

"I paid someone in Baghdad to accompany me. A fixer."

"All right, that's something I can believe."

"But you don't ask me enough questions, Saleh. Why?"

"Because I already understand why you are here."

"You mean why I have come all this way?"

"Yes. That."

"Then please, do tell."

"You needed to come to an end-of-the-world sort of place. This one just happened to be available. And it was for a good enough cause. Look at all the Yazidis and Christians those sons of Satan have killed. You wanted to do something about it. And you were already tired of your everyday life, wherever it was. I don't know what you did before besides being a journalist, but you had had enough. Like the rest of us. You came here, where you don't have to worry about anything except getting shot at and making tea for the fighters and having them call you Abu Faranci. That's enough to make you happy. I've been watching you, Mr. Claude. You are content here. I don't really know why a Frenchman needed to come all the way out here to find contentment. But you did. And I've seen stranger things in this world."

"Your English is better than mine, Saleh. How come?"

"I worked hard to acquire it. I thought it would be my ticket out of the Middle East. Instead it has been a ticket to stay here, in this prison. Then again, where would I go?"

Haji Yusuf had begun to sing the evening call to prayer. You could hear his crackly old voice with a hint of self-mockery in it radiating from the rooftop of the longhouse.

We sat there listening in the room I shared with Cleric J, and now also with Abu Faranci. Soon there were other calls from other abandoned, semihabitable buildings that the Hashd had taken over. The prayer calls got entangled in one another, like poorly tied knots that could not be undone. The better voices suffered the most for it and were lost. Every evening was the same. And every evening the enemy too sang his own *Allahu akbar* thousands and thousands of times over. We were really fighting with our own shadows. Some of us deserved dying, but very few of us deserved the flower of martyrdom.

The Frenchman's ease was compelling. He really did love it here. Every night all the men who had been lost to these plains and hills were recalled in our evening prayers. I prayed for them too. But there was no time to pause for them too long, no time to remember them beyond an idea. And so at the end of the day, all the martyrs you'd known became one bandwidth of death, a rainbow of body parts and browned blood. Sometimes at moments like these you just want to cry for your loss. It's a plaintive hymn of self-pity that I'd heard some men, but not all, descend into once in a while. And now I was feeling it too, especially since tomorrow morning I had to finally return south to Miss Homa and Proust, both of whom wanted their own share of martyrdom.

"But I wish to tell you about myself," Abu Faranci said.

"Huh?" My mind had wandered.

"You just described me in a paragraph, sir. But there is more to me than just my laziness."

"I did not say you were here because of laziness. But even that is a good enough reason for being here. I think this is why I am here, anyway."

"Ah! Maybe that is why I am here too. Do you know what *joie de vivre* means?"

"Yes. And I don't have it."

"When did you lose it?"

"I may have never had it. But if I did, I'm sure I lost it in Africa."

"Ah! I lost mine in America. Many Americans have much joie de vivre. It should be illegal."

"They make the rules. We can't tell them to stop being so enthusiastic."

"Well, we French try now and then to tell them. It is a mistake. We should not try."

I said nothing. I liked this guy. My idea of the French had always been the family my mother had married into after the old man died. The Francophone money of old Tehran, like that pseudo-cousin Avesta. They were of the class that turned their noses up at you for not knowing how to say *sympathique* with the proper accent. At gatherings they huddled among themselves and babbled in French and talked about the "lovely" party at the French embassy last week and then looked at you with expressions of utter pity when you tried to join in but weren't fluent enough to understand everything they said. That had been my idea of the French and France, except for a handful of hardened and gritty journalists and photographers I'd run into here and there. But this Claude fellow shattered all my preconceptions. I had expected a different man, full of himself and too suave. I was really waiting with my editor's eye for him to show me one mistake, just one, so I could throw the manuscript of his life into the dustbin. It would have been that easy. All it would have taken was a simple "I don't trust this guy" from me to Cleric J, and Abu Faranci would have been done for. It was a scary idea and it was the kind of power that one had in northern Mesopotamia at the time. But Abu Faranci had turned out to be the real thing. Our sympathies were mutual and I found myself wanting to protect him from the evil that lurked around us.

He said, "I had a family. Once."

"What happened? You lost your joie de vivre with them?"

"Not really. Rather, they found theirs. In America."

"Well, this should make you happy. No?"

He shrugged. "It did. I found a sort of happiness

in that, and then I left to come here." He stopped and looked at me. "Saleh, maybe you want to do your evening prayer first."

"Maybe you want to do yours."

"I haven't a prayer left in me."

"And I am running at least ten thousand prayers behind. I'll never catch up."

"Do you think the Middle East will ever find peace?"

"No. We should rather learn to live in it without peace but with civility."

"How is that possible?"

"Just like this, here and now. If a few weeks ago someone had told me an Abu Faranci was coming here to join our humble mokeb, I would have laughed at them. I might have even been insulted. But here you are. And we're talking. This is called civility, even if half of what we suffer here is because of you guys."

"Only half?"

"Yes. The other half is our own bad behavior."

The generators cut out and dark enveloped everything. Men's voices shouted in Arabic. It would be awhile before they got the electricity going again.

I said, "Claude, you've come here to die, haven't you?"

The dark allowed me to ask the question that was impossible to ask while looking into the man's eyes.

"Yes."

"Do you not think this is irresponsible of you? We cannot be the assisted-suicide headquarters of all the men who are tired of life."

"Why not?"

I'd never considered it like that. So it took a few moments for me to answer. "Because this is a real fight. Not a game. Our holy places mean something to us. What do they mean to you? Nothing!"

"It is all right if you wish to insult me."

The angry hum of the generators was already starting back up but there was no electricity yet. In that dark, with the sound of distant big guns walloping the ends of our minds, it was as if we were at the end of history too. There were at least three times in the past year I had felt this way: once when I buried that Proust book right here at the Eye of the Horse; another time when our positions were attacked at Tuz Khurma while Zahra the Beheader and I stood there holding her fresh bread, talking of Baghdad; and a last instance at Khaled's old place across the mokeb, watching the beautiful people of Hollywood on television.

Abu Faranci said, "Have you ever been married, Saleh?" He did not wait for me to answer but went on: "It is a beautiful thing, marriage. It is like an illumination. But, you know, betrayal changes the very atoms in your body. I know, in this darkness you are thinking, *This Frenchman has gone crazy and is giving me life lessons.* But I'm not here to give anyone any lesson. You wanted to know why I'm here and I am telling you."

"I am sorry if you felt insulted before," I offered.

"This is your world, your fight, your geography. I know I am an intruder. But I need an ear."

"Why?"

"Because I am trying also to make sense of this story of mine for my own sake. You are right, this mokeb and this war are not, as you say, places of assisted suicide. But I must ask you again: why not? At every moment, everywhere, something or someone is serving a purpose. Why should your purpose not also be to help me in my journey? This is my first question."

"But that isn't a question. It is a statement."

He was silent for a while, and I wondered if I'd offended the Frenchman again.

"You are right, Saleh. I did make a statement. But do you accept it?"

"That I—we—should assist you in getting yourself killed?"

"Well, yes!"

"Hang around here long enough and it will happen by itself. You won't need our help."

"This is all I ask for. That you let me stay. Thank you."

"You're welcome."

Silence again. Was he for real? It dawned on me that in all my encounters with people from his world, I was always the one asking for something—a job, a favor, a recommendation for a job, recognition of some kind. It was a one-way street of asking, even groveling, that men like Saeed and Mafiha had perfected to an art. Yet now, this man, Claude Richard, was asking me for something. A favor. The ultimate favor. And I had the power to give it. Or to at least not stand in his way.

"You have more to say, Claude?"

"Only this: by telling you something of myself, maybe I will be helping you too."

"Helping me?"

The electricity came back on outside, but the room stayed dark. Maybe the bulb had gone bad with the sudden surge; whatever it was, neither of us seemed to mind the circumstance. It was as if the Frenchman and I were speaking to ourselves, as if we had become one and the same person. I felt that I was in a trance.

He said, "Helping you, yes. To understand yourself as you think you understand me. I needed an honest war and I came looking. But I needed one to die in, not one to live through."

"Well, I'm not here to die, Abu Faranci. There's a difference between me and you."

"True. But you are here with the knowledge, because of the danger around us, that if you do die, it is for something bigger than you. This gives you a warm feeling at night."

"If you say so."

"I say so. And the rest of it, it has to do with that first thing I spoke of: marriage. I want to tell you about what happened to me after one of my trips when I came back home. We were living in New York City then. My posting as a financial journalist was there. But I had to go away often, leaving my wife and child alone in a land full of, well, enthusiasm."

Footsteps were coming toward us. I switched on the flashlight and shined it at the wall. The men might have liked Abu Faranci well enough by now, but he was still a foreigner. Sitting in the dark with him while the mokeb was bustling would make simple men skeptical. And they would take that skepticism out on him. Someone would. Maybe Maysam or Cleric J or Haji Yusuf, or any of the lesser guys in this place. The truth was that we were always a trigger away from some kind of destruction. We lived in the moment and it revealed itself in the sheer mountains of garbage we were able to produce.

Refuse sat all around us. Plastic and feces. More plastic and more feces. The transience of it all made us madmen. It is easy to misuse the word "mad," but madness on the scale I speak of can only issue forth in war. Or perhaps in violent revolution. It has no place elsewhere. And madness does not take kindly to the dark.

Maysam stuck his head inside and asked who was here.

"*Ana wa* Abu Faranci," I offered.

Just then the light popped on. A momentary blindness and then the three of us regarded each other. In Maysam's eyes was the look of the doer, the man who worries after others and holds the power of death and life. Without saying it, he still seemed to be saying, *It is not too late if you think this man is an impostor. We can stick his head under water, you know! Just give me the word.*

I said, "Abu Faranci wants to turn to Islam."

Maysam did not smile or offer a show of enthusiasm. He looked at Abu Faranci, turned back to me, and then his face seemed to say, *This is acceptable, and timely.* Then he was gone.

Abu Faranci said, "Maysam is the only one who still has distrust for me."

"He manages our security. It's his job to distrust. It's not personal."

I waited again. There were voices in my head. The last time I'd tried to get on the metro in Tehran, I imagined the oncoming train to be a tank, an Abrams to be specific—Americans. It had been at the Taleghani station and when I ran out from underground, just about suffocating, I came face-to-face with a guy selling pineapples right in front of the door of the former American embassy where they'd painted a death skull.

I hadn't tried taking the metro since.

"You look like you are sweating, Saleh."

I breathed. "Please go on. Your marriage."

"It was a good one. Nevertheless, the devil of infidelity was with me."

"You're a Frenchman."

"Oh please, Saleh! Let's throw away the clichés. I've come here to die, don't forget. I was not unfaithful because I'm a Frenchman. That is ridiculous. I was unfaithful because it was there like a fruit, and I was often away, and in a sense it came with the job."

"So you've come here to die because you were unfaithful? This seems like a heavy price to want to pay for something not that uncommon."

"No. On the contrary. I am here because on one of my trips home I found that my wife had also lied, cheated if you will. But before you imagine that I am here because my wife was not faithful, let me tell you that that was not it either. In fact, when I realized she was being unfaithful, it was as if I had been released from all manner of responsibility. I was suddenly free."

I thought of Atia telling me she was going to marry Mafiha. It wasn't the same thing. Not at all. But later on when I'd thought about it, I realized there was some form of twisted freedom in hearing the person you love tell you they will marry someone else. Once the dark cloud passes, you can settle inside your misery and let it rock you to desolate sleep.

"What did you do?" I asked.

"The man she was seeing had twin sons the same age as my own boy. He had been divorced for some time and owned a large home in the countryside where his former wife also lived nearby. The boys all went to the same school in the big city. It would have been a clean arrangement for all, except that the man's former wife seemed unhappy about a married woman playing mother to her sons. I could understand this, and I suppose so could my wife. Therefore, one day my wife insisted that I come to that big, beautiful American country house for a weekend visit. I was, in other words, a decoy, a distraction. I already knew that I was being part of a deceit and yet I did not mind. Because all these years I had been the one to be deceitful. It was a settling of scores and I was fine with it. You could say that in order to make my own deceit acceptable to myself, I engaged in another deceit, this time in collaboration with my own wife."

He sighed.

I did not like where this was going. Yet Abu Faranci seemed intent on telling his story and I was not going to get in his way—not so late in the game for us.

"It's a moment, you know, Saleh? It takes just that one moment to see all of life's truths arrange themselves in front of your eyes. And I saw it up there in that big, beautiful American country home. My boy was so happy there. It was as if he had two new brothers. I saw the joy in his heart. He had a family at last. And not just a gloomy Frenchman for a father who had wanted to be a war correspondent and instead ended up reporting about financial markets and trading in stock portfolios. Do you want to know when the moment came for me, the moment when I saw the light and knew I could walk away from everything without guilt, without remorse?"

"I am still sitting here listening, am I not?"

"Yes, you are. And I thank you. That American man

who had taken my wife, he had built a dirt track for motorbikes at his country home where he taught his children and my boy how to ride. I had, honestly, not a shred of envy in me watching him. He was so capable, so able to build and fix and be the kind of man I was not. He had, if you will, joie de vivre in abundance. True abundance."

"I guess that was good for your wife and son. No?"

"Yes. They had come under his protection. They too had developed joie de vivre. It was lovely to watch. But that moment, the moment I speak of, the moment of enlightenment, it came as I was taking a walk toward that dirt motorcycle track and I ran into my wife getting on the back of the American's bike. My wife said to me, 'We are going to the house to get dinner ready. Will you watch over the kids?' Those were her exact words. Here I was in America, a land that I did not particularly like or dislike, in the house of a stranger who was sleeping with my wife, and I didn't mind it at all. And I thought to myself: *My God, Claude, what a waste your life has turned into!* And I saw the joy in her face as she got on the back of that bike with him, a lovingness that I had never seen before with me, a joy that I was seeing in my son's face too every day in that big country home. It was then that I knew the time had come for me to leave."

I could not bear to sit in silence after a confession like this. So I immediately asked, "And then you hurried here to get yourself killed?"

"No. It took awhile. First the divorce. Then the man's former wife creating some kind of trouble. Something about custody and things of that nature. All the little things that can make life unbearable. But in the end, it all worked out. I put my life in order. I quit the monotonous reporting job. I did my research about where to go. And, well, here I am tonight speaking to you."

I wanted to ask him about his child. For a second I even resented him for his child's sake. But it wasn't my business to push him. Plenty of the men who came here to die were fathers and even grandfathers. I had known more than my share of them. I'd just never thought I would see a man so far from our world wanting the same exact thing. Never considered it a possibility. Abu Faranci may not have been typical in that way, but he wasn't an impossible character either. His road to the Eye of the Horse was just a bit different than the other men out here. And I understood that anything I said to him now would be preposterous. Therefore I kept my mouth shut. And together we headed out into the evening.

12

The next morning we went south. A caravan of usual suspects, plus Abu Faranci, heading first to Tal Abta. There was a gas station there where Cleric J had business. After which I assumed I'd be passed on to another Hashd convoy heading to the capital on my way to link up with Miss Homa and Proust. The countryside was a flat nothingness. Occasionally on parallel dirt roads a dot moved and we didn't know if the thing was ours or not. Nothing was taken for granted in victory. Because victory had been here before. And it always managed to slip away. Like fish. Or happiness.

We drove in three trucks, hardened men who breathed retribution and the diesel stench of war and loved it. I sat in front next to the cleric, taking in the murderous smoke of cigarettes that only he and I seemed to not care for, the vehicles putrid with a staleness that is indescribable. If I survived, I would live out my life remembering hours such as this, when breathing seemed pointless. My eyes tried, and failed, to catch the distances where a drone, a plane, a gunship, an enemy suicide truck, a friendly, or really any motherfucker at all who could spook you out of your melancholy might suddenly emerge. But my eyes were lemons, God-given failures that mostly just guessed at the things men spoke of

when they pointed into distances and felt for the placement of their weapons.

Names. Everywhere there were names, so many
combatants and hangers-on and lost souls treading the
dying misfortune of Mesopotamia that one got lost in
the maze of titles and martyrs and those waiting in line.
I had developed a fear of returning to the places where
war was at a respite or nonexistent. Though dangerous,
Tal Abta was still a few kilometers too far away from the
action; I would rather go back to our mokeb and wait for
the enemy to strike again. It would have been suicide on
their part to hit us once more, but suicide was their stuff
of life. And somehow I held the unreasonable faith that
if only I stayed at the mokeb long enough, all the dead
would return as if they were ghosts on a catwalk.

In the designated gas station just south of Tal Abta, a
row of men sat looking like they had just been refused
their mothers' milk.

Cleric J said to me in Persian, "Saleh, today is another
day of justice."

I faltered. "But I have that ride to catch to Baghdad."
I reminded Cleric J that the roads were clogged with
refugees. I had been assuming that my new ride would
be another Hashd truck with its flags, bullhorns, and
general mania. But now I was told I'd be going with a
"civilian" vehicle. This meant long waits at roadblocks
where any car ahead or behind might turn out to be a
final call.

"Turn on your camera," Cleric J commanded. "Record everything."

Maysam and Haji Yusuf and the rest of the men

fanned out through the gas station. When a car tried to enter one of the platforms, they directed the driver away. I sat in a corner and trained the lens on the men who had been sitting there before we arrived.

Cleric J went into a lengthy monologue about the nature of justice. After a while I lost the thread of the words, as the convoluted Arabic became enmeshed with my own thoughts of home and my mother and Atia and more martyrdom.

Cleric J stopped talking. There was a long, awkward pause, and then one of the men began his turn. He was a big man, maybe as big as Maysam, and spoke with the deference and I-eat-dirt voice of someone who has known shame. It became apparent he was the oldest brother among the men sitting with him. He spoke of the blight in their family, the disgrace, and that whatever Cleric J decided, his word would be law.

"Your brother took ten thousand American dollars to buy sheep for a brother of ours in Samarra. Instead, well, you already know what happened. In times like this, when we all should be as one, is this the correct path or the path of the devil?"

The man's voice shook. "I wish I could kill him myself."

"No need for that. When does he get out of prison?"

The man looked at his brothers. He knew. But didn't have the heart to say. And his saying that he wished he could kill the jailed sibling with his own hands was not true. The pain in his face was shame multiplied, threatening a heart attack. I had stopped wearing diapers after Syria, but now I wished I had one. The camera shook in my hand, the cell vibrated (Atia from Tehran). And now I glimpsed the man who had confided in me last night,

Abu Faranci, standing at the edge of the road from the gas station looking south. Again I wondered if he at least missed his son, if not his marriage.

Cleric J, seeming to be a whole other man than what I'd known these months and years in and out of combat, spoke in a low voice and gazed at the floor somewhere between us and the four brothers. "I will tell you when he will be out. He will be out tomorrow morning. At eleven, to be precise."

None of the brothers spoke.

"Now then—"

The man interrupted him with a loud clearing of his throat. "We disown him. We haven't a brother. He is yours to do as you deem just."

"I know I speak with honorable men here," Cleric J offered, "or we would not be talking."

There was a loud murmur and one of the brothers began uttering a *salawat* which the others and Cleric J and even I immediately picked up.

We grew silent again. The air remained heavy. We had done the salawat and dutifully remembered the Prophet and the family of the Prophet and somehow that absolved us of . . . what? I didn't know. My mind was wandering some more. Now I thought of Atia and Mafiha having a child together someday. It did not bother me, this image, not as much as I thought it would. Maybe there was truth to the words from Abu Faranci—getting to the point where even your wife's or husband's faithlessness becomes a nonissue. I felt for him, for Abu Faranci. As I felt for the men in front of us about to give up their thieving brother to the take-no-prisoners justice of Mesopotamia.

"We are indeed honorable men," big brother said

forcefully, willing himself to believe his own sacrifice and the sacrifice of his tribe.

Cleric J cleared his throat. "He must die. You understand?"

All said it together: "Understood."

"But, brothers, countrymen—yours is a tribe known for its courage and its respectability. It is not our intention to bring disrespect or shame to your history. This is not the way of the men of Iraq."

The more he spoke, the more his Arabic fell into a classical baroque that I could not understand. I felt dislodged, as if standing on air.

Big brother said, "The men of Iraq must stand together, after all that we have been through."

"Then you understand that what your brother has done, his betrayal, calls for it."

"Death!"

"Death."

"So be it."

"But, my fellow Arabs, if tomorrow or the next day someone in the tribe should waken and feel that retribution should be meted to those who meted retribution, then—"

Big brother cut in: "No such thing will take place."

"The human heart is willful and unpredictable."

"Our tribe is at your command. What do you wish from us?"

"Your word, on your honor and the honor of your tribe and your ancestors, that the matter will end upon the justice handed to your brother and that there will not be an extension of this feud."

"*Allah!* There is no feud. This will end with the end

of a man who is no longer our brother. He is disowned for his infamy."

The stillness was the quiet of the sater on nights when you imagined you could feel the hot breath of the enemy upon you. All these months I had thought Cleric J was doing me favors. And he was. But favors have a price. I had been brought here for a reason.

The men stood up. Kisses on the right side of the cheek and shoulders followed. They walked quietly to their trucks and drove away. The gas station was ours.

Cleric J turned to me. "Be that as it may, Saleh, I cannot allow any of my men to do the deed. This tribe is strong. Some young hothead might take upon himself the thought of revenge. Then there will be no ending to this blood on blood. You understand, yes?"

"What are you telling me, sayedina?"

"You have a chance to redeem yourself for not exacting justice on the North African. You do recall the North African, yes?"

"Allah is my witness, yes."

"You are not from here. If you were to carry out the punishment, it would end with you. It would finish here tomorrow when the man gets out of prison."

I put the camera down. "Tehran is not Sweden, sayedina."

"Explain!"

"They can get to me easily over in Tehran."

"What then? What do you suggest I do? Have one of my own men draw blood?"

As soon as he'd said it, his attention went to the window and outside. I followed that gaze until both of us were staring at Abu Faranci.

Cleric J said, "That man came here to die. He told me so."

I nodded. "Is that why you brought him along today?"

"I was not sure you would take the call, Saleh."

"Why were you not sure?"

"You are not the kind of man who takes the call. You only want to be near the men who do. There is a difference. Your commitment is to something other than commitment itself."

It was a mild affront and I accepted it because it was true. I looked again at Abu Faranci, Claude. What was he staring at so intently on the horizon? There was nothing out there. Emptiness. Death. Dirt. Sand. Wind. Rolling scrub and bullet-ridden concrete walls.

"But is this justice, sayedina?"

"It is not injustice."

He walked past me. It was as if Abu Faranci had expected him to come his way at this exact moment. Men stood rooted to their designated spots, weapons in hand, looking on; it was not unlike watching a gangster film unfolding in the last place on earth. From where I stood all I could see with my half-good eye was Cleric J's bobbing turban and Abu Faranci's stone face. Then Abu Faranci reached to take Cleric J's hand, then pulled him forward and pecked him on the right cheek twice.

Jasim asked, "And what did Abu Faranci say to that?"

Jasim and I sat across the table at a new café that had cropped up by Ridha Alwan's in the Karada District. Before leaving for Baghdad, my last words to Abu Faranci had been to tell him he didn't have to do what was being asked of him.

"Abu Faranci said I was wrong. He said he had to do it."

Jasim grimaced. "And you said . . . ?"

"I just repeated to him that he hadn't signed up for this sort of thing." *Oh, but you are wrong, Saleh, I did sign up. For all of it. There was never a choice.*

On the road, Jasim stayed silent for too long. It was unlike him to be so subdued. He meant to put me on one of the buses near Baghdad Airport heading for Najaf. We drove and after a while the sea of people walking, sitting, eating, crying, beating their chests, mourning and celebrating and loving Imam Husayn, got to be overwhelming. They were all heading in the same general direction so they could get on with their walking pilgrimage. There is something beautiful and unlikely about the "walking pilgrim," the kind who just walks and walks—the entirety of her purpose to prove to herself, through pain, a love of the martyr. I had come across walkers as far north as Samarra who were lost and searching for the Askari shrine while there were still reports of enemy snipers two kilometers away. A busload of Iranians had gone up in smoke in a suicide attack just the other day on the way to Karbala and still they came. They came no matter what. They walked like there was no tomorrow. And truly, that was the point; there may not be a tomorrow because our Messiah, the *Mahdi*, might suddenly appear after all. One had to do the walking while there was still time. I'd been to two previous Arbaeen pilgrimages, but all of a sudden this sea of humanity—which would only become a thousand times worse as I got closer to Karbala—appeared impossible to wade through.

"I can't do it, my friend."

"You cannot do what?"

"Go to Karbala. I'm sure Imam Husayn understands. I cannot face these crowds. I'm no good. I have been no good for a while now."

I reached over and held Jasim's wrist as it went to shift gears.

He looked at me. "Are you all right, Saleh?"

"I'm not. I've been seeing things lately. I was in the metro in Tehran and I imagined the train pulling into the station. It was a tank. I was sure of it. I had to run out of that station. I haven't been able to go inside the metro ever since. Have you ever stared down at the barrel of an American tank, my brother?"

"Saleh, you know I have. More than once."

As if on cue, the phone buzzed and there was another call from Atia.

When I still didn't answer, she wrote: *You must call me. Much news.*

Bad? I replied.

She did not answer. I turned the phone off. Thought about it, then turned it back on.

When I looked up, Jasim had pulled over. An old woman, hands outstretched, came to his side of the car and he gave her a couple of bills. Crowds were milling in the street. It was impossible to drive. A group of wailing Iranians walked a few meters ahead of us singing about martyrdom completely off-key. The lead singer was a burly Azeri Turk who slid between Turkish and Persian with songs about the valor of Imam Husayn and his companions. A boy ran to the car from a makeshift mokeb and handed me a sherbet. All the loving of the world was in that little boy's face. He'd been taught that during Arbaeen you had to be generous and serve. I took the sherbet and turned to see that Jasim was crying.

"Why are you crying, my brother?"

"This land. It kills me."

"I know. Me too. All of it. The bad and the good. The evil and the saintly. It's all killing. Killing and killing!"

"That woman . . . that woman you left with me, Saleh."

"Zahra," I said, and then reluctantly added, "the Beheader?"

"Her, yes. I am sorry I was not more careful. You put her in my care and she's dead for no good reason."

"Many people are dead, my friend. We can't let it destroy us."

"Some dead hurt more than others. She was no one to me. But she was my charge. She had eaten of my salt and rested her head in my home. She was my guest. Do you know what it means to lose a guest?"

I was feeling awful enough, but Jasim was taking us to a far more existential place. I had a feeling we'd both have a mental breakdown right here if we were not careful.

"You have a beautiful family, my friend. You've lived through hell. Everyone in this country has. You don't need to make yourself more crazy with things that can't be helped. Zahra the Beheader probably wanted the end she received."

"Do not be cruel like that, Saleh. You know no one wants that."

"I'm just trying to let you know it wasn't your fault."

"It was. Many things are my fault, Saleh. Many things. I have endangered my family. I am ashamed."

"What are you talking about? You've done nothing but provide for a whole tribe, not just your wife and children, your whole big extended clan. I'm witness. I know. Who has been bringing in the bread if not Jasim? Everyone knows this."

"That is the trouble. Everyone knows."

"Everyone knows what?"

"That I worked for the Americans for a while."

"So? It's not a crime. A lot of people did."

"Yes, and they're dead."

"Those were informants. It's different."

"They were not. They were men like me. Translators. Fixers. You know my type. Why do you think I've had so little competition these past years? My competition died!"

"Stop this foolishness, Jasim. No one's going to kill you. Those days of revenge are long over. The Americans are mostly gone."

"You think so?" He snorted. "A time of peace gives people more unoccupied hours. They have more time to think and make themselves crazy."

"Well, we don't quite have peace yet. So you are all right."

He smacked himself hard on top of the head. "I'm a fool. I should have never worked for the Americans. I should not have translated even one sentence for them."

I was getting irritated and concerned. I'd never seen Jasim like this. "So what do you want to do?"

"I must leave this country."

"Have you lost your mind?"

"Saleh!" he pleaded. "Don't you understand? They have put the word out. I've been threatened, marked.

It happened last week. You already know what that means."

The phone vibrated. It was Proust. I patted Jasim's shoulder as he cried quietly to himself. Somewhere in the past minute, with him falling apart like that, I realized I had to pull myself together. Between my own troubles and now Jasim's, I was even more certain I could not face the crowds down south. There were easily tens of thousands of mokebs like the one I had been serving at down there. But they were not resting stations for war; they were for peace and love. The difference was in size. I was comfortable up there in the north where there was war, my world circumscribed, my schedule neatly fitting into the dawn-to-dusk timetable of soldiers and killers. I knew who the enemy was and generally where he was. And I knew there was no salvation for any of us. It was just the fighting and, yes, the revenge, and the occasional dying. I could handle that. This, the goodness of people, their hopes, their prayers and perambulations, their carrying themselves by the boots of their souls to get to the shrines of Imam Husayn and his brother Abu al-Fazl in Karbala to pray and revitalize their faith, this I could not handle. It was beyond me. It was too big in scope.

I said into the phone, "Proust, I cannot meet you and Miss Homa in Najaf. Impossible!"

Proust softly spoke back: "Saleh, you don't have to. We are not in Najaf anymore."

"You are in Karbala then? Are you at the shrines?"

"No. We are in Samarra and hope to come north. We are coming to you."

They were already farther north than I was.

* * *

Grand mosques are humbling experiences, like grand churches. They are bullies. It is the little mosques, rather, that warm a traveler's soul. The small, makeshift excuses that are merely functional, marked with the sweat of refugees and the destitute, reeking of shoelessness and longing.

Jasim and I sat in one at an outer ring of the mechanics' quarter of Sadr City. Ahead of us was a graveyard of cars as far as the eye could see. Across the road a man and his two assistants were busy converting an old, decrepit tractor into a homemade Hashd armored vehicle to be sent north. The trifling faded-blue dome of the mosque was pockmarked with bullet holes and words. Men with missing feet, legs, hands, arms, eyes, and ears sat around praying or quietly talking. Once in a while people showed up with offerings of food for them. They were veterans, these incapacitated men, having fought in recent wars or old wars—now with no one to care for them except the folks in the mechanics' quarter.

Beforehand, we'd stopped at Jasim's home nearby and taken his little boy and girl out for ice cream. Their innocence was like fresh air. I thought of how during long stretches at the sater, you no longer remembered there's a world of children in the back somewhere. Unlike Iran, Iraq was a country swarming with kids, in every street and alleyway, yet you'd forget they existed at all. Just as you tended to forget that half the world were women. You ached for them distantly and not in a sexual way. They were your mothers and sisters and beloveds and they were not here. Not one. The setting of the men of the Hashd turned desire inward until it was extinguished. You bottled it up and threw away the key until the next time you were, say, in Baghdad or Amman. And then, in an instant, just the mere sight of an ankle could throw your world into disarray. You remembered who you were. You were not a ghost.

I said to Jasim, "Your children will flourish and you will live. Stop worrying."

"How can you be so sure?"

"Like I said, the time for revenge is over. So you did a little work for the Americans back in the day. A lot of people did. If anybody wanted to get you for that, they would have by now. Someone's playing a stupid joke on you. They want you to feel some heat. It's your job to try to figure out why."

I left him to that thought for a minute and stepped outside. A man without legs was perched on top of the shell of an old white Toyota which itself was perched on top of several other car shells next to a garage full of broken wheels. There was no way to explain how this legless man had gotten up there, but there he was, as surely as I was here now watching him watch the make-shift mosque. He was the illness and hope of this land. I knew that as a reporter I'd never be able to quite convey what I saw here. Yet I didn't want to take a picture of him either, as easy as that would have been. For the same reason I could no longer go south to the Karbala pilgrimage. I was tired of photos and photographers capturing pilgrims as if they were coins in a piggy bank. Miss Homa must have taken one look at that landscape and seen the same thing. Death would have diminished returns alongside several million walkers having their pictures taken all the time.

Smoking a cigarette, Jasim joined me outside. Our eyes rested on the legless man.

I said, "Look at me and my partner Saeed, we worked for all kinds of people. In fact, you were the one who brought a lot of those jobs for us. But no one's threatening us with death for working with infidels, are they? None of it matters now, Jasim. Someone is playing with you. That's all."

"And I should take it easy because it is only a joke? Would you take it easy? I have a family. You just saw my little ones."

He had a point.

He went on: "By the way, what happened between you and Saeed? Why do you no longer work with him?"

"Never trust a man with a camera, Jasim. His loyalty is always to his contract."

"You are telling me this *now*? It is my job to work with men of that sort. It's how I make my living in this terrible land."

"And look at where it got you today!"

He turned and stared at me. "Thank you for making me feel so much better." He spat and walked to his car.

"You're welcome—and I'm sorry!"

I closed my good eye and the world was soft again. I was back in Khan-T in Syria in a pothole with Nasif waiting for the enemy to make a move. I was with Moalem writing in his tedious diary. I was with the Afghans coming back to the red house to show they were not just fair-weather friends. I was with Atia going to a widow's house in the Abdulabad District of Tehran to ask for the widow's hand on behalf of a comrade who had already been killed a day earlier.

Atia picked up on the second ring.

"Saleh, our mutual friend says that State TV is not accepting the ending for the *Abbas* show. Their exact words: *Abbas, the great sniper of Iraq, cannot be taken down like that by a common enemy sniper, and a woman at that.* Audiences will not accept it. Nor will State TV accept that Abbas falls in love with a female enemy combatant."

"Then tell our mutual friend and State TV to go to hell."

"Our mutual friend also says that once you have finished with the business of a certain French book and its owner, if you don't go to Erbil for that other business, whatever that is, he will have to send people after you."

"Tell our mutual friend that once he is in hell, he should remain there."

"Where are you, Saleh?"

"In a graveyard of hopeful car parts."

"I have one piece of good news though. Two, actually."

"You are going to have a child with the boss—and they are twins!"

The silence was painful. And now I saw the legless man slide down the car shells with such ease, and with a cigarette in his mouth, as if he had natural glue on his palms.

"I'm sorry, Atia, for my bad behavior. I think it's called jealousy. Or maybe defeat. Maybe both."

"The *boss*—Mafiha, my husband, your friend—has rid you of your problems. He spoke with State TV. And they told Saeed he had better withdraw his lawsuit against you regarding the *Abbas* show, if he knows what's good for him. They are committed to you being the original creator of the series."

"All they want in return is a happier ending for Abbas, right?"

"Of course."

"Thank the boss for me."

"He also took care of that other lawsuit against you."

I had already forgotten that Avesta, my pretend cousin, intended to sue me too for the article I'd written about his theft of Miss Homa's ideas.

"The painter guy. Your cousin."

"My so-called cousin!"

"The new magazine has decided to commission a long article on him. You don't have to do a thing. Mafiha will write the article himself. The lead piece in the art section for our second issue."

It was too clean an ending for it all. And it was classic Mafiha. Just taking care of business with more business.

The legless man had disappeared and the guys turning the old tractor into an armored vehicle were swearing, livid about something. Apparently their oversized gadget's turret was stuck and wouldn't turn.

"Any chance your husband could fix my issues with our mutual friend as well?"

"You know that's beyond his scope."

"I guess there are still some things the great man cannot do."

"Saleh!" Atia's voice was forceful. "You need to call our mutual friend. In fact, you need to get back here as soon as possible."

"What's for me there, Atia?"

"A visit to your mother's grave, for starters."

"Nane-Saleh is gone?" I closed my good eye and tried without success to see her.

"Are you all right, Saleh?"

I imagined this place without a war. Just men casually missing limbs and other men turning a piece of farming equipment into a killing machine.

How did it feel to execute someone? It was an insight that Abu Faranci would possess by now.

"Atia, tell our mutual friend I will go to Erbil for him. I promise."

"Saleh!"

"And thank your husband for arranging my mother's funeral. I'm sure he's the one who took care of that too. I know he's really doing all this for you. But I'll take it. I owe him in a big way. I'll even read his peace poems and try to like them. I'm not saying this with irony. Honest!"

One of us hung up.

Beneath some hard-to-make-out Arabic graffiti on the battered vault of the mosque, someone from somewhere had written, in concise and nearly immaculate Persian: *A mountain will never reach another mountain, but a man will reach another man and take his revenge . . . if he must.*

It was a variation on an old saying. The original Persian proverb said nothing about revenge. Whoever had written those words had some precise ideas about what they wanted to do. And you could have summed up this land in those words.

Miss Homa lay in bed in the back of a barbershop near al-Alwa Square, a short walk from the Askari shrine. Her eyes were closed but she was awake and Proust held her wrist, crying quietly. Jasim waited in the car outside. The barbershop was a two-seater and pilgrims, all of them Iranians, were lined up against the wall waiting for haircuts. From their beaten appearance, you could tell they were the kind of tireless wanderers for whom a simple march to Karbala was not enough; they had to come this far north and had walked past Baghdad all the way to Samarra to show their true worth as walkers. You'd see them on the side of the road, looking haggard and monumental in their great revel of sacrifice. They were beyond reach and reason, like exquisite skeletons. I imagined some of them reincarnated as Christian martyrs nailed to a rock and weeping ecstatic tears of blood. While others came on buses and didn't walk at all, suggesting that they were complainers and a potential nuisance in their excessive wants.

The chaos of it all was infectious. The look of trance, and rapture, in the eyes of a pilgrim who has trekked a thousand kilometers is worth being born into this world for.

I walked over to Jasim.

He said, "I may not see you again, Saleh."

A dusty wind had picked up and the town seemed under a barrage. So much had happened in the years since the Americans had come and gone. So much wasted blood, all the destroyed mosques. The enemy had been relentless on Samarra, swooping in from the horizon in their pickups and black banners, waving their atrocity in our faces and rubbing it in. We had been losing then, but the cordon for holy Samarra had withstood the assault, barely.

Evil was still in the air, however, and this dusty wind had a smattering of that time.

"You had best get going before the road to Baghdad is closed."

"Saleh, you haven't asked me why I may not see you again."

I did not tell him that a man can only take so many goodbyes. I was exhausted. Mostly with my choices. And those of others. I met Jasim's eyes and waited for him to speak again.

"I will take my family and go to Morocco. I worked there before. I have connections."

"Jasim, Morocco is not Iraq. They don't need translators like you over there. You'll be bowing all day and night to French and German tourists. You'll be a waiter in some tourist-trap restaurant."

"So be it. Do not be harsh on me, Saleh. I cannot live in fear for my family here every day. Look at what happened to . . ." He trailed off.

"Zahra the Beheader?"

"Ay, yes," he said in a way that was not quite his own Iraqi accent, as if he were already considering himself gone from here.

"God be with you, my friend."

"And them?" He pointed toward the barbershop.

"I guess I will not have to worry about a haircut in Samarra."

"What will you do with them? That old lady looks very sick. She needs a doctor. And that young man, he . . ."

"Looks confused? That he is. He can't go back to Iran."

"Why not?"

"They already named a street after him. He's a martyr."

Jasim raised an eyebrow. "They think he died in battle?"

208 ⊘ Salar Abdoh

"Something like that."

"And you are here to do what for him?"

"He believes he should become a real martyr and not remain a fake one."

"But Saleh!"

"I know, my friend. You have to escape to Morocco and this man, I suppose, has to do what he has to do."

Jasim thought for a bit. "I could take him to Morocco with me."

"You are too kind. I'll figure something out for him. He will not die. Not if I can help it."

"Allah!"

"Allah!"

Jasim disappeared in a squall of dust and traffic.

Back in the barbershop, the old guy cutting the pilgrims' hair was making fast work of his clients. He was an austere believer with a square, unsmiling face. His green skullcap slanted a bit to the side, making him look slightly comical with that Moser shaver moving like an orchestra conductor's baton in his hand. I knew him from earlier passes through Samarra. After they had pulled his nails out and burned his tongue with scalding water, he had eventually become part of the sea of Iraqi refugees who escaped to Iran during Saddam's reign. He did little but cut hair with an efficiency and single-mindedness that made you a believer in regular visits to the barber. I was not sure how Proust had known to come to him, but here we were and it was as good a place to be as any.

Miss Homa's eyes were open, staring at the ceiling, when I came back in. She turned to me. She seemed pleased about something. In her weakness, she was also strong. As if illness had given her a reserve of strength and I had to play catch-up before she expired.

"Saleh, you are here." She smiled again, a weak smile full of compassion. "I guess this gives a whole new meaning to 'appointment in Samarra,' doesn't it?"

Proust sat on the chair. He had cried himself into silence. I had never felt so sorry for this land as I did just then. It was one of those sentimental "why us?" moments that can make a man turn his face up to the sky and start an irrational conversation.

"You will be fine, Miss Homa."

"She will not!" Proust yelped, suddenly wanting to pick a fight.

I glanced from him to her. Then I took out my cell phone and wrote a message to the last number I had for H: *I have our Proust.*

H wrote me back right away: *What do you plan to do with him?*

Keep him in Iraq. Like you ordered.

I went closer to the smallish, uncomfortable-looking daybed to get a better feel for Miss Homa. Proust sprang to his feet. He had become her protector.

"What happened?" I asked, addressing both of them. "Why did you two come all the way up here?"

"She wanted to walk with the pilgrims," Proust volunteered.

"Yes. But this is not Karbala. You didn't just walk seventy-five kilometers. You walked three hundred! What were you thinking, if I may ask?"

Miss Homa eyed me gently. "It's what I wanted."

"She caught a cold," Proust said quickly. "She caught *something*. An infection maybe. Maybe it was bad water.

She refuses medicine. Made me promise not to call you. She kept walking. She will not eat."

"Son!" She reached for his hand. "Is this not why we came here?"

That did it. Proust was off again, crying. The three of us like lost baggage from a shipwreck in that sea of humanity that was the Arbaeen pilgrimage of Iraq.

"But why Samarra?" I asked again.

Her breath was light but she spoke clearly. "We decided to come to where you were. To where the war is. The pilgrimage was fine. But it was a carnival. It was not what I wanted. This is as far as we got. I could not go on."

Proust added, "And the roadblocks north of here wouldn't let us."

"I could get you a doctor," I said to her.

She dismissed my suggestion with a wave of her hand. "Saleh, do you think the Mahdi, our hidden Messiah, really vanished right here in Samarra? Do you think when he comes back he'll reappear here after a thousand years?"

"We don't know, Miss Homa. All we know is his father died here."

"A place of mysteries then, Samarra."

"I did not realize you believe in these things."

"It's never late to believe, Saleh. It's like being asked for a dance. I always liked to dance when I was younger. I'd like to believe my paintings are dance."

The barber stuck his head in the back room, his green skullcap like a vintage attachment to his body. He gave a nod, grunted, and retreated.

I knew the color of death. Miss Homa would die tonight. Or tomorrow. Or the next day. She was paler than ever. She had made sure to squeeze the last of life out of herself during this pilgrimage. I'd sometimes see it with other pilgrims of her age too. A sort of counting down until the light went out, as if they were here to secure a spot for their own funeral march. And in doing so, they became angels. She was glowing. That familiar glow above the head. The glow I'd seen on all the martyrs up and down this country.

At dawn I opened my eyes at the foot of the Askari shrine. Somebody had stuffed my shoes under my armpits while I was asleep so they wouldn't vanish. Later, when I looked in at the shop, the barber had gone out and in his place Proust had taken up the Moser to cut the hair of the pilgrims. He seemed to be doing just as fine a job of it too. Two days passed like that. Our non-talking barber, Proust, me, and Miss Homa in a town where our Messiah may or may not have disappeared for his centuries-long absence. Tradition had it that when he returned, none other than Jesus Christ would be accompanying him. The two of them together would set the world right again.

Meanwhile, we waited.

This was a peaceful interlude that I didn't want to violate by calling north to see how the war was going. The war was not going anywhere. I'd get back to it soon enough.

I tried to get Miss Homa to eat, but she would not budge about her fasting. Proust retired into himself, and would only occasionally take up the slack for the barber. The barber had a name but I cannot remember it now. Sometimes it seems that it is only the names of the dead

I can recall. The living being immaterial. Miss Homa wasted to nothing by the hour and the barber appeared to understand perfectly why we were here. He asked no questions. We were his pilgrims. He would not deny us. A woman had come to die in Samarra. This to him was as good a reason as any to be in Samarra.

"I have put all my affairs in order, Saleh."

"I know. You have already told me these things."

"My paintings. Everything. After I am gone, you will give notice that I have departed. Then they can dig each other's eyes out over the prices of my works."

Proust came back from a visit to the shrine sometime on the second day. He had a book in his hand. It was Spanish poetry that had been translated into Arabic. I knew he could not understand enough Arabic to read with ease, but it appeared to have been the closest thing to his heart that he could dig up in this place. So I left him with his poetry and his sulking and waited for Miss Homa to die.

She died on the third day around noon. Three hours before, we had been chatting about the martyrdom of Imam Husayn and she had told me of her special love for Imam Husayn's brother, Abu al-Fazl. This was the man who had given up his life for the imam and his thirsty companions while trying to fetch water through enemy lines.

"Do you think it's wrong to love Abu al-Fazl as much as Imam Husayn, Saleh?"

She was descending into a state of semiconsciousness and delirium. She had not had a religious bone in her body most of her life. Now she was comparing her love of Imam Husayn and Abu al-Fazl; it was the kind of transformation you don't know whether to be suspicious of or admire.

I held her hand. "It's all right to love Abu al-Fazl like you love Imam Husayn."

She smiled and did not say another word after that.

It was a Wednesday, I think. Proust was cutting hair next to the barber. His knack for the job was impressive. His book of Spanish poems lay by the sink, dog-eared on a page with a poem titled "Y Nada Importa."

And Nothing Matters.

The new cemetery of Samarra was a straight shot down the road. The barber had already made arrangements. I left a sizable wad of money on the dresser for him.

Noon prayer would begin soon.

I had expected Proust to weep. But I never saw him weep again. Nor did he take his book of poems along. He left it for the barber and his shop.

13

H wrote: *Our terrors don't always match the dangers that inspire them.*

It was the second time he had sent these words. Now I was sure he had lost his mind. There is something not right with the world when the man who is supposed to be your interrogator, your anchor, your nemesis, starts to get overly literary. These men should be the bastions of equilibrium. A steady ship in their occasional cruelty. What had happened to H? What did he want from me?

Proust and Abu Faranci had become inseparable. Sometimes they spoke in whispers, in French, for long hours. They also went from somberness to occasions of downright boisterousness that were out of character for both. They would, for instance, join the Arab men in their nearly daily routines of one-upmanship in the impromptu war-poetry slams. It was breathtaking, the Arab predilection for verse at any moment anywhere. Standing there watching Abu Faranci and Proust at those times, I had to wonder what was going on in each man's mind. Did Abu Faranci truly not think about his son anymore? Was this it for him? And what of Proust? Miss Homa had only just died, and Proust had seemed to reach some sort of an end with it. Yet now it looked like he had fresh lease on life next to Abu Faranci.

In all this time I never broached the subject of what Abu Faranci had done about Cleric J's request at Tal Abta. He'd carried out the execution, I knew that much.

It was his business.

The mokeb itself was in a bit of a lull, though the smell of some looming battle was not far. It came from the north and the east, and sometimes even from the direction of Syria. A few times we caught groups of enemy men coming right up to the Eye of the Horse, probing our defenses, looking for weakness, trying to figure where to hit. I did not know of the information that the interrogation of such men brought, and capturing them alive, I imagined, was still rare here. They were rabid things, consummated with a purpose that could make you question your own resolve and spirit.

At the same time there was also an inner stirring and a sense of reckoning. It was time for Cleric J and his men to pack it in for the month and go south. But they were staying put. The capture of Mosul still seemed a long way away. Yet we had our slice of the war and would be damned to abandon it for flatbread and olives back home.

I finally wrote back to H: *Do you not think that your usage of cell phones is detrimental to your occupation and well-being, seeing that you are a bona fide representative of our distinguished republic?*

H: *No need for your cynicism, Saleh. I have many phones. It is one of my occupations.*

Me: *What is it you want? I am certain you are not writing to me about Proust (I do not mean the writer and his book, but the man I have here with me).*

H: *No, I am not writing you in regards to him. Just have him remain there. They'll send him some money and new identity if you tell me this is required.*

Me: *Why do you care so much what happens to him?*

H: *Shouldn't I?*

Me: *It's actually a beautiful thing that you do care. But it surprises me.*

H: *Without people like him and you, I would not have the job I have. I am a reader. This is a blessing.*

In all this time, I had intermittently thought about that other "enemy." Not the enemy that faced us right here at the Eye of the Horse. And not the Americans who were not really an enemy but more of an apparition and a nuisance, by turns obscenely generous and then stingy, and then generous again and without a comprehensible mission in Mesopotamia. This, rather, was the enemy that I had never seen in flesh and blood. It felt that the scholar had written that first e-mail to me ages ago. I opened my e-mail account and saw that H had been using it to be in touch with her. The back and forth, from his end, was written in questionable English. He had invited her to Erbil: *Erbil is free territory Madam. Is safe. No danger for everyone. Even you come with good passport. No problem. Good food. Come here and I see you first. Then I research for you Jewish places in all old Tehran.*

She had said yes to that, not even bothering to ask why she would need to come to Kurdistan to meet me before I did some basic research work that anyone could do in Tehran. The e-mails had gone on for another several rounds and she had given some dates she could get away from teaching. I sat there, in my little mokeb room in Iraq, reading e-mail exchanges of Interrogator H pretending to be me. I did not know what H's madness entailed for him to do this. And one can throw the word "madness" around too easily. But there was something most definitely reckless in H's behavior.

Proust and Abu Faranci were outside my room; I could hear Abu Faranci teaching Proust a French poem. Others had joined their duo and everybody was trying to imitate Abu Faranci's French. It was heartbreaking, and sublime. And I wrote to H: *What is this Erbil business? What do you mean to get from it?*

H: *Out.*

Me: *You are mad.*

He quoted again: *A woman who you love rarely satisfies you completely. So you betray her with a woman you don't love.*

Me: *What in Imam Husayn's name does this mean?*

He did not answer and I didn't press it.

Outside, I heard a blast. It was deafening, and while the window to my room with Cleric J remained intact, the rest of the windows nearer the mokeb entrance were shattered.

I ran outside, following Proust, Abu Faranci, and the others toward the thoroughfare to see the damage.

What had happened was that the old man with the sheep who'd pass by the mokeb at least once a day, sometimes twice, had finally blown himself up. The only casualties were him and his sheep. He had been a good hundred meters off before the vest he was wearing detonated. For an hour sheep entrails lay about the road while convoys squashed it all into a diminishing soup. There was not much left of the old man. We didn't know who had put him up to it. It appeared he may have detonated early on purpose or there was a malfunction. It put you at a stinging unease, this. The Eye of the Horse was mostly a militarized town. For someone to come right up to your doorstep and blow himself up like that made every precaution seem worthless.

I walked back to the mokeb to busy myself with feeding the men. I had to shut off my mind. For the next few hours I did nothing but cut frozen chicken and make rice to feed a thousand boots.

Before the call for evening prayer I finally looked up to see Abu Faranci standing there watching me. Apparently he'd been there for some time.

My arms were exhausted from negotiating pots you could cook a whole goat in.

"What?"

"You have barely talked to me since you came back from the south, Saleh."

I shrugged.

"Are you unhappy about what happened at Tal Abta? Maybe I didn't carry out that execution, you know."

"You did. The men told me. I don't care how you did it, if that's what you want to talk about."

"I did it with a bullet. How else would I do it?"

"You should be very proud of yourself then, Claude. Welcome to our world."

"It's war, you know. People die."

I stood up and got right in his face. He had aged. Literally aged in a matter of days and weeks. As if he'd been here doing this for many years. This story was winding down and I wanted to hit Abu Faranci, and mostly because I cared for him.

He had managed to make himself a part of our myth. I did not begrudge him that. I begrudged him his absence of indecision, the lack of uncertainty. He hadn't come here to write dispatches for anyone.

I begrudged him his conviction.

"You've proved yourself. Go home now, Claude. What you did was not part of the war. It was personal business between Iraqis."

"I don't agree with you. When there is war, everything is war. All the wheels that turn."

"Go back to your wife and child. Do it before it's too late. They will come for you."

"Who will come for me?"

"The man's tribe."

He smiled. "My wife and child are no longer mine. They are another man's. You know this very well. You are angry with me for something that I do not know. I do not understand this anger you have now."

Proust came toward us and stood at a respectful distance. Haji Yusuf let out a few rounds of AK at the tea stand on the other side of the thoroughfare near Khaled's old place. I knew it was him by the way he exhaled his rounds—it was a *tat*, *tat-tat*, *tat-tat-tat* burst that made me think of my old bike's sleepy exhaust on a winter day in Tehran.

I turned to Proust, speaking Persian: "Have you told this man why you are here?"

"*Bale*, yes."

"What does he say?"

"He says every reason is a good reason."

"What language does he say it in?"

"French."

"You discuss literature?"

"Often."

I pushed past Abu Faranci who now stood there silently listening to our incomprehensible Persian.

"Do you think about Miss Homa?"

"I try to keep myself busy so I don't think at all."

I patted Proust gently on the shoulder and kept walking, heading for my usual spot at the mokeb roof.

Abu Faranci called out: "I was sure that old man with the sheep would blow himself up one day."

I stopped and turned. "Why not say something then?"

"I did not know when he would do it. If I said something, they would question him and he would never do it. Then I would look foolish. People would say, 'Abu Faranci thinks he knows more than us.'"

"You were worried about your reputation?"

"I was worried the old man would do something worse after that."

"But how did you know in the first place?"

"The old man looked desperate. No one watched him. I did. I understood him. He came and went, came and went. Like a clock. No one was watching. But he was watching. And I was watching."

I said, "I paid attention too. I saw him."

"Then why did *you* not say anything?"

"No one would believe me. I am not an expert."

"Then you understand my silence."

I did.

The mokeb roof was often as close as I could come to solitude.

Below, they were all there, on the other side of the road around a little bonfire, warming themselves, drinking tea and eating dates, stretching their limbs, glad that they had all of their limbs, glad the old man hadn't killed anyone but his animals and himself.

I wrote to Atia: *Miss Homa is dead.*

It took a long time for her to answer. More than an hour. And then all she wrote was *What?*

Dead, I repeated.

Atia: *Where are you?*

Me: *She died in Iraq. In Samarra.*

Atia: *What was she doing in Samarra?*

I could not help it: *She had an appointment.*

Atia: *Saleh!*

Me: *Tell your husband the news. He can be the one to break it. It's a scoop. Tell him if he has money, which he does, he should buy whatever he can get his hands on of Miss Homa's. Price doesn't matter. Tell him to borrow money if he has to. Because after the news, tomorrow or the next day, her prices will double, even triple. He can sell then.*

Atia: *Saleh!*

Me: *Tell him these exact words: Miss Homa made sure there are not too many of her works left for buying. She gave them all away to charity or destroyed them. But there are still a few left here and there. Tell him to go to anyone selling her works and pay any price they ask for before he breaks the news. If he can hold onto what he bought for even a few months, he can sell it for a fortune. Tell him! All right? I'm your art guy, don't forget! I know about these things.*

Atia: *Saleh!*

Me: *This is my way of paying your husband back for all his help. I hope we are now even. And I pray you have a wonderful life.*

She tried calling, but I didn't answer.

I wrote to H next that I was ready for Erbil and asked him what exactly he wanted me to talk about with the "enemy" scholar once I met her there. He didn't answer. Two hours later, when the weather went from chilly to downright cold, I was still sitting there waiting.

My Iranian data plan was dwindling fast. I could tell by how slow my phone was getting. I did a sluggish crawl through the Western papers to see how the war was going according to them. As usual, they didn't disappoint. There were several pieces about the Afghan fighters and how the Iranians were using them as mercenaries and giving them citizenship in return for their services. I thought about my Afghans in Syria, especially of that moment when they all ran back into the red house to support us, afterward kissing me and Moalem like we'd been their long-lost fathers. Later still that night: how we all stood in two rows at a special prayer with Moalem leading, speaking the same mother tongue, and later somebody opening a page of Hafez and reading it out loud, then someone reciting a verse by Rūmī, and finally calling it a night with something from Khwaja Abdullah of Herat. I wanted to shout through the ether of the Milky Way and set the record straight. I wanted to explain about Hafez and Rūmī and Khwaja Abdullah and ask the world: *What the fuck do you know about Khan-T and the Afghans and the red house? What do you know about the Arab warriors still standing there by Khaled's old house, warming their hands on this chilly night in Mesopotamia with little more than the shirts on their backs and their ancient Kalashnikovs?*

I wrote to the enemy scholar: *Madam, I can meet you in Erbil exactly two weeks from now.*

I had created a new e-mail address for myself and apologized to her for having to take extra precautions. I asked her not to write to the old e-mail again. I gave her a precise location at the Lengeh Souk in Erbil's old town, where resourceful Syrian Kurd refugees had ended up running small businesses. They also ran excellent coffeehouses, better than anything the local Iraqi Kurds in Erbil could manage.

By early the next morning, when she still hadn't written back, I knew she wasn't coming to the coffeehouse I had designated. This had been another case of "chasing after black peas," as the Persians say, and I had no idea what H had meant to do in Erbil with this enemy scholar. But I had wanted to go there anyway. If for nothing else, just to get away from the mokeb for a while—to go to a hotel bar and order a shot of anything and drink it without dread and without anyone's judgment.

Meanwhile, Proust insisted more than once that if he were to die, I must take him back to Samarra and bury him next to Miss Homa. He liked to talk about himself in the past tense. I said yes to his request though I never intended to make good on it—not because it pained me, but because I was lazy. And it all really depended on how a man went; if it turned out to be a case like that old man and his sheep, then you'd feel stupid collecting meat parts off the earth to go bury them a couple of hundred klicks down the road.

When H still didn't answer after several attempts, I figured his lack of discipline and general predilection toward high art and Marcel Proust had finally cost him something. Maybe his freedom. Or maybe he was already in Erbil or somewhere else trying to escape this rotten Middle East forever. I waited one more day. Neither of them wrote, neither H nor the enemy scholar.

In return, I did not answer Atia's calls and messages,

not even when she reminded me I'd better soon come up with that new ending for the *Abbas* show for State TV.

More eventless days. No casualties. No captures. The mokeb was running itself with Abu Faranci and Proust and the other guys. One night I dreamed of the Kurdish combat women over in Syria and suddenly I had the end of the *Abbas* show in sight. He would not be felled by an enemy sniper whom he had fallen in love with. But rather, he would save a platoon of Kurdish women, his occasional allies and occasional enemies, depending on the time of the year in Mesopotamia. He would put his body and his soul in between them and the enemy as they approached the heights in which the Kurds were trapped. The greatest sniper in Mesopotamia would make one last stance to save the women. He would not be killed by one woman; he would die for many. Heroically. Rapturously. This melodrama, I thought, State TV surely had to accept.

I was back to being a writer, even if what I wrote was questionable at best, and hackwork at worst. I didn't want to think about that.

I spent most of the following days cooped up in that room, rewriting and periodically listening in on the chatter of the mokeb, its poetry and its occasional French.

They hit hard at first. It was around four p.m. I had my back against the entrance of Khaled's old place and counted three rockets coming down just up the road where the sniper squad used to bunk. My pristine table of tea and sugar in plastic cups, waiting for the afternoon warriors en route toward the border, did a backflip and then everyone was running. We of the mokeb were just Friday fighters who happened to be here every day, and suddenly the town seemed unusually exposed. I was frozen. It was not that I was unable to move or that I was shitting in my pants. Nothing like that. It was a perfect freeze inside my body, as if I had swallowed a man-sized cylinder of ice. Now the coffee man came hobbling this way. His small, tribal coffee mokeb by that old snipers' billet was dust. This much I was certain of. But as he passed me I was not sure if the next thing I saw was my imagination—he seemed to have only two dusty stumps for arms. His kaffiyeh blood-soaked and dangling barely off his neck.

My irrational anger of the moment had mostly to do with my ruined tea for the men. I saw stars and turned deaf. One of the several Muhammads from the mokeb was shaking me and screaming in my face and I swayed back and forth to the strength of his passion.

I was dumb. Frightened into a version of courage. We were running, in circles it seemed. And for a brief moment it appeared as if the attack was coming from every which way. It wasn't. They were only in front of us. We were not flanked. There was not a bloody thing to flank anyway. There were no pickups or APCs, just men on foot, not more than two or three specters that popped in and out of buildings like paper targets at a gun range. It was outlandish, gamelike. Yet many of the men from the mokeb did not even possess weapons. Troop movement had been concentrating on the west for two days, toward the general direction of Deir ez-Zor in Syria where the enemy was making an all-out play for the city. There was fear they might blitz us too from that direction. I thought that absurd, because we all knew they could not spare the manpower to move back into Iraq. They were spent, the sons of bitches. They were trying to get *out* of Iraq, not back in it. But you could not argue this fine point with Friday commanders and fighting clerics who, after all, only meant well.

Now, as I write these words, fully conscious of my ignorance of all things martial, it might appear that I know what the fuck I'm talking about when I discuss the things that happened. I don't. I have shot a few weapons in my life. But it was always as a guest of the weapon. Not its master. And I never hit anything that I intended to hit because my eyes would not cooperate.

It was no different now. Emptied of the random platoons that made up the Hashd forces in this ghostly place, the isolated mokebs suddenly found themselves on the perimeter of a battle that should not have happened. In the last few days we had thought this geography finally cleared of the enemy, their last suicides taken down at the threshold of the Eye of the Horse a week before. Maybe there would be pockets here and there—and not so close—that would eventually be flushed. But nothing like this. I wish I could give a minute-by-minute account. But mostly I was just searching for a lens through which I could have a modicum of vision.

I saw him, that familiar stance of the guerrilla with an RPG that I'd last encountered at Khan-T. Here: a dusty roadway with occasional battered buildings on either side. You could have imagined two cowboys suddenly appearing from behind their respective walls to face each other and you would have been forgiven the mindfuck cliché. Because that was exactly what it looked like. I closed my left eye to see better, or see period. There he was in that disheveled hatred of his, several buildings down in the direction that the coffee man or the coffee man's specter had just hobbled from. Cleric J saw him at the same time and screamed, "*Down!*" which we all obeyed because he was our mother and our prophet.

That man could have killed every one of us. Instead he chose as his target the emptied mokeb. I don't know why he did that. But God bless him! Then his backup followed with another round into the smoking mokeb. They must have had information that that was the place they should hit if they wanted to score a major body count.

An instant later, Maysam took one of them down with a clean shot, just as Moalem had done in Khan-T. The ground shook and the fresh rattle of vehicles from the fuel depot gave us hope. We had backup after all. Maysam started gathering the men, and once the two armored engines were on the dust road, we all hung back behind them, scared buzzing flies that we were, and slowly walked toward the destroyed coffee mokeb and the ruined sniper billet.

Maysam and his men fanned out in front of the second building where we'd seen the targets, while I stayed with Cleric J, Haji Yusuf, Abu Faranci, Proust, and several of the men who didn't have weapons. Arabic escaped me then. It was a language bristling with heat, concentrated and heroic, reaching my cottony ears in surges like staccato elegance from the Koran.

The enemy was "scissored." They'd retreated inside the one-story building that had lately been used by the local quartermaster. I knew what Cleric J was thinking. This was going to be our new mokeb, because our

228 ⌇ Salar Abdoh

old one had just turned to shit. An argument ensued. Maysam was giving signals to take the quartermaster's building down with the engines, but Cleric J wanted the place intact. He was being unreasonable. We could carry our seared onions from the destroyed mokeb a little farther up or down the road; there were plenty of desolate buildings to choose from. But Cleric J wouldn't have it; he had no time or patience to sweep for explosives in a questionable building before we inhabited it.

We were not going to pound these bastards; we'd flush them instead.

Then he ran. Cleric J, limp-dashing toward that building to show us schoolchildren what it meant to be a fighting cleric. He was, as always, setting an example. For isn't it said in the holy book that *no fear shall be upon the friends of Allah*?

He ran, and then Abu Faranci and Proust ran after him.

I've tried ever since to hold onto this moment. Investigate it. Try to understand its contours. The moment when men and women choose courage (perhaps a better word would be sacrifice) at the expense of survival, which is everything. I already knew nothing would happen to Cleric J. When you have spent enough time with a guy in a war you get a feeling if he'll go down or not. I never saw that halo of the martyr over Cleric J's head. I never feared I would lose this mad guardian-angel cleric.

Now he did what he always did, turning around and screaming something to us that was his version of *charge!*

Abu Faranci and Proust stayed right with him.

Our turret swung right to left, pointing above the

heads of the three men. Out popped the enemy, his legs standing a good meter apart, as if he were drunk or had something precise to prove about how much of this earth he could cover in his last moments.

His shots, wild and random, missed Cleric J, who was hobbling on his prosthetic leg, and instead found Abu Faranci square in the neck and shoulder.

In return, the machine-gunner's volley lifted the man off his feet and pounded him back into the building. It was like he had been trying to catch a ball just beyond his reach that went right into the next world. I watched Cleric J and Proust slowly crawl toward Abu Faranci. A pool of blood had already formed around him. I didn't move. There were more random shots, but it seemed to be clear. Maysam and his men stormed the building belatedly and a few minutes later they came back out carrying only the upside-down black flag of the enemy. Uncharacteristically, since it had God's name on it, they threw the black flag to the side of the road, and not without some disgust on their faces.

Men came from the north side. Our guys. Clearing buildings one and two at a time. The engines and Maysam's men moved to join them but I still didn't move. Haji Yusuf, excited as always, was shouting things I only half heard.

Proust didn't have a scratch on him. I stood back and watched him staring at Abu Faranci's dead body. Cleric J was murmuring something; perhaps he was saying a *fatiha* for the dead Christian.

Later, when we were situated just as Cleric J wanted in

the quartermaster's place, Proust came up to me while I was cooking the Iraqi rice noodle dish the men loved so much.

"They buried him like a Muslim."

"The man was righteous," I said noncommittally without looking up.

"Saleh, I don't know what to do next."

"You were counting on being dead. I know."

"But I'm alive."

"Seems that way."

"When then?"

"I'm not the angel of death, you know! Besides, you made a good try. You ran right alongside Abu Faranci. No one will take you for a coward here. I can't say the same about myself. It could have easily been you instead of him."

"Do you not feel his absence?"

I glanced up at him finally. I had expected, when the time came, a more intense battle. Something at least mildly heroic. Something that would earn Abu Faranci the gold standard martyr status. But it didn't really matter, because they were calling him a martyr anyway. And that was all he had wanted. Or maybe he didn't even want that.

No one would know he'd been here—no one outside Iraq and the orbit of our Hashd lives and deaths. When I followed the news of all the people who were joining this war from far away, those delicious stories took place elsewhere and belonged to other people—and that was just as well for us. Yet I knew that Cleric J had already made sure news would head south to the tribe of the executed man: a certain Abu Faranci is dead. The revenge narrative would stop with him. The equation was complete. It would not go beyond that.

Proust said, "Why did you not come to say a prayer for Claude?"

I had not wanted to hear the names of the dead. I'd drunk a lot of coffee from the hands of that coffee man. If he was dead, I didn't want to know. If he was alive, I didn't want to know. And if he was wounded beyond recognition, I still did not want to know. I wanted, in general, to stay ignorant of many things now. I didn't want to get to know people and then have them die on me. It was better; the flights of despair came less frequently that way.

I said, "I've been praying for Claude all night. He was . . . a complicated man. I am sorry we did not get to know him more."

"What becomes of me?"

"You'll have to stay here. Try not to die if you can. This war's ending. There's no reason you should do what Abu Faranci did."

"Stay in Iraq? Really? Forever?" It was as if he were pleading his case.

"Do as you wish. Go back to Iran if you like. They'll think you're a ghost."

"Please don't mock me, Saleh. You know that return for me is impossible."

It was. And it hadn't escaped me that with two major works of Miss Homa to my name, I'd be a rich man when I got back to Tehran.

"You can stay with Cleric J in Diyala for now. I'll arrange it. I will send money your way from Tehran. After a while you can join the sea of refugees from this war going to Europe. Head for France if you can, your first love. Take long walks in Paris. I always wanted to go there. Send me a photograph."

14

You can lose everything. Refugees know this. But so too do people who live their lives in photographs. I had many pictures of this war. One war among many and one I tried in a roundabout way to write about. Because it was there.

It wasn't long afterward that one day I woke up back in my house across from the synagogue in Tehran and realized my computer and all that was in it had died—like Abu Faranci at the Eye of the Horse, or like my lost cell phone before it. All those photographs and videos taken by a half-blind man—gone!

I could reach out to the living (and I did) to retrieve some of the images—photos others had taken of us at places like Khaled's billet. Shots taken with cell phones through cracked, battle-beaten screens. Certainly many of these images were circulating around. The ether didn't let it all go up in smoke. But my own images, the ones I'd taken with my own hands, they had disappeared for good from one day to the next.

This didn't make me question what we did and if any of it was real. It was. All of it. The proof is in the everlasting posters of the martyrs. Or at least as long as the martyrs are still honored in posters and photographs. Because they too may one day go up in smoke. In mem-

234 ⌒ Salar Abdoh

ory, just as they did in body. Then what? At nights I lie awake and watch the synagogue chandeliers and think about such things. Because I haven't even a war to keep me busy now and away from the demons of peace.

Abu Faranci's death put a damper on us all. Cleric J gave us a variation of a sermon on loss. He said that it was debatable whether we could call Abu Faranci a martyr. Who knew why he had really come to us? But come he had, and he'd done more than his share. Therefore we had to honor the man, but only in our memories and taking it no further than that. There was a practical reason for this, Cleric J reminded us again. If we brought news of his death beyond Iraq, somebody would surely make a case against us. They'd say that we had murdered him. Because this was what they always said about us. How could we explain (and who would do the explaining?) that Abu Faranci had been among the best of the righteous. He had served and fought valiantly. And when the call came, he had given his life. Abu Faranci was one of us. And we would recall him the way men recall those who have taken a bullet for their brothers: we'd keep him in our prayers.

Nevertheless, his death was the closing of another chapter. The enemy had tried, desperately, to make another "last push" in these parts and failed. It had been a ridiculously low-level fight and when it was over we'd sat around wondering what the point of it was.

So the war would go on, but not here. It made us feel disrupted. When I told Cleric J that I had to go to Erbil on some business, he did not protest—even though in his mind the city of Erbil, firmly situated in the sphere of influence of our uncertain allies the Kurds, was an eventual battleground.

I went back to Baghdad and from there flew to Erbil. I took a hotel room and every day for four days visited the coffeehouse at the hour I'd asked the enemy scholar to come. She was a no-show and I'd figured as much.

I drank.

The second day, as I was drinking in the Ankawa District, I saw a Kurd I knew from three years earlier. He had been part of the bodyguard detail of a man I'd tried to name, in a dispatch, the "kindest warlord in all of Iraq." The Censorship Department in Tehran, naturally, had slashed the entire sentence—in fact, the entire paragraph. The warlord was a brave old rotund Kurd who had fought Saddam to a draw in another lifetime and had had to live with wolves, so he said, in order to do it. This former bodyguard of his was a poet at heart who had been caught too many times writing instead of being alert. The kindly warlord had let him go so he could be a poet instead of a warrior. And now I was seeing him four tables across from me, scribbling away deep in his notebook, the world literally at his fingertips, happy, content in his art at last. I envied him his happiness. And I was not even sure why, besides the drinking, I had come to Erbil at all.

I went back to the hotel and for the very first time tried to look up this enemy scholar online. I hadn't done that until now because I'd been afraid of what I might find. Maybe I'd find nothing and realize it was all a hoax and that Interrogator H was testing me as usual. But there she was. Smallish and with the graceful face of a reader. Her steel eyes seemingly lit up the camera, her smile intelligent. I did not want her to be my enemy, or anyone else's enemy. Why had she not written back? What were we to each other but two people riveted by the same universe?

I came across a few photos of her backpacking somewhere by the Sea of Galilee some years earlier. The pain of losing Atia was now confused with the sudden love I had for this person whom I'd never met and, I knew, would never meet. So for the next two days, while waiting senselessly for her to show up at the coffeehouse at the souk in Erbil, I had visions of us in an alternate life. Married with kids and happily backpacking around all the troubled lakes of the world. I imagined long nights of heated political argument that ended in heated lovemaking and toasting to the spirit of all the martyrs of all the wars around us.

And then my four days were up. Without love, only with messages from Atia that said the going rate for Miss Homa's works had already doubled and people were clamoring to know where she was buried. I knew she was not saying any of this in a mercenary fashion. She just wanted to provoke some response out of me and probably figured this was how to do it.

Saleh, the news said there was a major battle around where you are.

At the end of it all, the only justifiable reason for going to Erbil had been to put more money into my Iranian SIM card—something I could not do from the Eye of the Horse. After Atia's text, I trawled through the Iranian news sites and saw that "major battle" was exactly how they were reporting the sad excuse of a fight that had taken Abu Faranci away from us.

By the time my ride dropped me back in front of our new mokeb at the quartermaster's building at the Eye of the Horse, I knew what awaited me there: word had it that Dodonge, now truly the sole superstar of the Syrian front, had come to report about our "major battle" in Iraq and its aftermath.

I pulled my winter hat tight over my face and observed the new mokeb from the side alley. The place was like a painting: men cooking rice in the open space in the back, chopping meat, stirring lentils, unpacking bags of vermicelli; there were fires being lit, poetry being sung, prayers being sent for the afterlife; and somewhere there in that huddle of men and song there was also Dodonge with a cameraman trudging after him as he spoke to soldiers eating food and telling jokes.

I could not step through that threshold. I couldn't do it. Instead I backed off until I was standing in the middle of the dusty road where just the other week two lost souls had taken a crack at us by pointing their RPGs toward the right target at the wrong moment. A truckload of men came barreling by, their stone faces tired. I don't know which sater they were coming from or how long they'd been there or where they were going. In my mind I called them war flies—expendable, solid. Maybe they were heading for Syria. Or home.

Khaled's place looked like a ruin. It hadn't been hit. But it had gone unused and smelled foul. I was sure that since the mokeb had moved up the road, men came down here only to use the place as an outhouse. As I stepped through the door I could discern movement. I stopped and waited for my weak eyes to get used to the dim light inside.

I hadn't noticed that the guy was already standing, staring me dead in the face—the way men do when they don't know whether to turn savage or ask for mercy.

He didn't have a weapon. Or maybe he did but was out of ammo and didn't care anymore.

In a reversal of the very same situation, I recalled the Quds commando I'd met in Tehran who told me he'd jumped up abruptly with his empty weapon, making himself a perfect target and counting on the enemy shooting first and asking questions later. He hoped to get enough bullets in him to not have to experience the ordeal of a slowly cut-off head. They'd obliged him and still he'd survived. This was called luck.

Sometimes it happens.

The thin-faced man grunted something about being *ta'baan*, so tired that he was just resting here. I grunted back wordlessly as if to indicate I understood.

I still can't be sure who he was and to which side he belonged. Maybe he was just a coward, or another poet who wanted some downtime away from the crassness of war. Even as I walked away I had already convinced myself I'd done a good deed that day. It's amazing how these little fabrications can help you go on.

And I wanted to go on.

15

It was inevitable. An *Abbas* sequel. This was the brain-child of Saeed, who ended up collaborating on it with State TV. I didn't begrudge him that. And the series became an even bigger hit when Dodonge, because of his so-called war expertise on the enemy in Syria-Iraq, was taken on as a "consultant" to the show. The show, however, was really a prequel—the life of Abbas before he became known. A young Abbas, in other words, showing the precociousness of his early years growing up in Basra before becoming the tragic sniper superhero of Mesopotamia.

The war for me was over—even though it continued in pockets and in fits and starts and promised to move on to other frontiers with other volunteers. I am back to writing occasional art reviews for my beloved Atia's new magazine. I do it for her, not because I have to. It is as if all of us had somehow found our rhythm through the martyrdom of distant others. Mafiha, for one, did another tour of the major cities of Europe with his peace poems; by the time he came back, he had already made good on the tip I gave him about Miss Homa's remaining works and scored a killing on flipping two paintings. With the profit, he now runs a gallery on the recently fashionable-again Sanai Street, where they have literary evenings and workshops on the second floor. I have an open invitation.

Atia will be a mother soon. My own mother I visited just once at the Behesht-e Zahra cemetery. I laid flowers on her grave and played five minutes of an episode of a Turkish soap through my cell phone for her. I would not visit her again.

Yet the dead howl to be remembered and the living accommodate them. Perhaps once a week I search on-line and see old friends—Haji Yusuf, Maysam, Cleric J—posting what now seem like ancient images of a recent war that is already threatened with oblivion. Once in a while in these posts I run across someone I have known who has been newly martyred. Maybe their vehicle went off road and hit an unexploded device; maybe they were taken down by the few remnants of the enemy who still lurk in the shadows. It's these fresh ends that really rub one the wrong way. They grate against the reality of everyday peace and make you suspect that what you did was of absolutely no consequence. The only thing worse than losing a comrade is losing them dumbly postcombat. This is what I told Interrogator H the other day over a cup of coffee. He is back at his station and in fact never left it.

I asked him, "Why did you want me in Erbil? What did you expect to happen there?"

"The ocean is big and one tries one's hands at everything."

"Are you a philosopher now?"

"I always was."

Then he asked about Proust.

He knows that I sold the earlier work Miss Homa

had given me and finally enjoy a comfortable life. I sent enough money through Cleric J to provide for Proust to join the Syrian refugees en route to Europe. He was almost robbed and killed twice and nearly drowned once, but he finally made it. He now lives in Marseille and has streaks of blue in his hair. I do not know why he is in Marseille and not in one of the designated refugee camps in Germany or Austria. I told him to go to France and he obliged. That is all I know. His status is still unclear and he may be deported yet. What is he to tell the authorities in Europe? That he cannot go back to his country because they'll think he's a ghost, a martyr returned from the dead? For now, at least, he remains with blue streaks in his hair in the land of his beloved namesake. And he's content with that.

I told H all of this and asked, "Are you not sometimes afraid of having to answer to your superiors for your highly unorthodox ways?"

"I interrogate culture, Saleh. They are a bit lenient with regards to my specialty. Besides, no one can touch me in relation to you. You are considered one of the Defenders of the Holy Places now. You are not an enemy of the state. You belong. Don't forget, you also wrote the original *Abbas: Sniper Legend and Fist of God*."

There was a sneer in H's voice when he said this, as if he were telling me I smelled bad and that this was good. In return I didn't tell him that I had taken it upon myself to supply that faraway enemy scholar with the information she wanted about the old Jewish ghetto of Tehran. After a while I even became something of an authority on the fabled Pamenar District in south Tehran, with its little alleyways and remnants of the Seven Synagogues lane. I put together a nice collection of photographs and archival material for her and sent it all from the new e-mail address. It took a month, but she finally wrote back: *Thank you.*

It was elegant, this simple note from her.

Nowadays, whenever there is a feast at my own synagogue across the street, I stare at those chandeliers, close my right eye, and allow my left eye to become a dazzle of colors and shooting lights. It is at times like these that I remember our ghosts up and down the breadth of these lands. And I especially remember Miss Homa, whose canvas of the dome of the sublime Goharshad Mosque stares back at me on my wall as I gaze through my opaque vision at the sky-blue door of Haim Synagogue and those tall chandeliers inside. I will never sell this second painting. There is much speculation about where Miss Homa really is and if she is even dead and if all of this is not just some ploy to drive up her prices. One person behind these false rumors is none other than Avesta, my "cousin" who stole Miss Homa's ideas and who has seen his own prices plummet ever since news of Miss Homa's passing hit the market.

I keep my silence.

It's all I need to do.

Because the business of the living is always too immensely turbulent to stop at anything for long. As early as next week, for example, one of the martyrs foundations to which Miss Homa left a number of works is holding an auction of three of her paintings. The auction, naturally, is to take place at Mafiha's new gallery where the richest men and women of the city have been invited. On the surface, the proceeds will go to the families of the martyrs, particularly those who left behind young children. But, of course, a good half of the take will be skimmed right off top by the people who run the foundation, with another 15 to 20 percent to the auction house. This leaves only a fraction of what Miss Homa originally intended, and there is bound to be a fight over that sum too. You could say that this is inexcusable.

But no.

It is an acceptable loss—like a broken and brave Frenchman, minus his joie de vivre, finding immortality at the Eye of the Horse.

TEHRAN NOIR
edited by Salar Abdoh
336 pages, trade paperback original, $15.95

BRAND-NEW STORIES BY: Gina B. Nahai, Salar Abdoh, Lily Farhadpour, Azardokht Bahrami, Yourik Karim-Masihi, Vali Khalili, Farhaad Heidari Gooran, Aida Moradi Ahani, Mahsa Mohebali, Majed Neisi, Danial Haghighi, Javad Afhami, Sima Saeedi, Mahak Taheri, and Hossein Abkenar.

"A tour de force not to be missed."
—*World Literature Today*

"This entry in Akashic's noir series takes the gritty sensibilities born out of American film and fiction to Tehran."
—*Publishers Weekly*

"*Tehran Noir* is not only a solid crime collection, but an illuminating look into day-to-day life in the Middle East, with religious and political implications galore, as well as racial tensions bubbling just beneath the surface . . . The stories in *Tehran Noir* aren't always easy to read, but they are engaging in the extreme."
—*San Francisco Book Review*

"The 15 stories in this collection also come from a stellar and diverse cast of Iranian writers . . . A collection such as this is able to bring Iran to life for the foreign reader in a way other fiction and non-fiction cannot . . . Superb."
—*PopMatters*

"*Tehran Noir* will prove fascinating reading to anyone with an interest in Iran. It will be equally intriguing for a reader who is simply curious about a theocratic society in the 21st century, or what became of a vibrant, cosmopolitan society after the fall of its dynastic ruler."
—*Gumshoe Review*

CPSIA information can be obtained
at www.ICGtesting.com
Printed in the USA
JSHW050542130522
25737JS00003B/3

9 781636 140322